The Little Swineherd
and Other Tales

Other Books by Paula Fox

.———.

The Eagle Kite

Western Wind

Amzat and His Brothers

Monkey Island

The Village by the Sea

Lily and the Lost Boy

The Moonlight Man

One-eyed Cat

A Place Apart

The Slave Dancer

Blowfish Live in the Sea

The King's Falcon

Portrait of Ivan

The Stone-faced Boy

How Many Miles to Babylon?

The Little Swineherd

and Other Tales

PAULA FOX

Illustrated by

ROBERT BYRD

Dutton Children's Books • *New York*

Library of Congress Cataloging-in-Publication Data
Fox, Paula.
The little swineherd and other tales / Paula Fox;
illustrated by Robert Byrd.——1st ed.
p.   cm.
Contents: The duck and the goose——The little swineherd——
The rooster who could not see enough of himself——Circles and straight lines——
The alligator who told the truth——The raccoon's song.
ISBN 0-525-45398-9
1. Children's stories, American. [1. Animals——Fiction.   2. Short stories.]
I. Byrd, Robert, ill.   II. Title.
PZ7.F838Lt   1996   [Fic]——dc20   94-39227   CIP   AC

Published in the United States 1996 by Dutton Children's Books,
a division of Penguin Books USA Inc.
375 Hudson Street, New York, New York 10014

Designed by Amy Berniker
Printed in Mexico   First Edition
1   3   5   7   9   10   8   6   4   2

For Robert Lescher

P.F.

For Jennifer, Rob, and Tracy

R.B.

Contents

The Little Swineherd
and Other Tales

The Duck
and the Goose

One fall afternoon, a duck, who made his living in show business, was waddling along the edge of a pond talking to himself. "Never trust chickens," he muttered. "Nor cats either!"

A homeward-bound blue jay lighted briefly on the branch of a nearby willow tree. "It was all your fault!" she jeered. "It wasn't my fault!" protested the duck. "I'm only a manager. How can I help it if my performers go berserk onstage? And how could I have known that cat was going to make such a beast of himself?"

"Your fault! Your fault!" shrieked the blue jay, flying off.

What injustice! thought the duck. Who else in the whole country except himself cared about discovering talent? Who else provided the animal community with glorious hours of entertainment?

He had thought he had a good thing in the cat. No one had ever seen a cat juggler before. And that cat could keep a dozen eggs flying in the air for five minutes without breaking a single one—although he had managed to swallow an egg once before the duck could stop him—and he could also balance six apples on his head while doing the Argentine tango. The duck had hoped he would make enough profit from the cat's performances to ensure a comfortable winter for himself. But, he realized, he *had* made a little mistake holding the cat's debut in the old barn where the audience was mostly mice. And perhaps he should have made sure the cat had had his supper before going onstage. That much he would admit. But he couldn't blame himself for what the dreadful creature had done—eating up his own audience, one by one, even as they were applauding!

He supposed he would have done better in the long run to have kept the chicken act. What could have been safer than a trio of singing hens? Perhaps he should have rehearsed them once before present-ing them to an audience. Yet how was he to have known they had been fighting among themselves for weeks about which one was to sing the solo parts? Of course, they'd continued their battling right up on the stage. A few rowdies in the audience had thought *that* was the show. But the rest of the animals had demanded their money back.

The duck was hungry. He didn't know what to do next. He might even have to give up being a manager and try a steadier profession. "I could clean barns," he said to himself, and wiped away a tear at the thought of such a disappointing end to his dreams.

At that moment, he happened to pass a clump of tall reeds, from the middle of which issued the sound of a low, sweet voice. The duck had no place to go, and he was grateful for any distraction from his melancholy thoughts, so he drew closer to listen.

The voice continued, and the duck was able to make out what it was saying. Something about a donkey and a beggar and a magic loaf of bread. A fairy tale, he guessed, some creature telling its children a fairy tale before bedtime. . . .

An idea struck him. Why couldn't he become the manager of a storyteller? A nice, quiet creature such as this one must be, with a nice, quiet voice? The tale was ending. "And the beggar was never hungry again, at least not for long, and the donkey was never mistreated again, at least, not very mistreated." The voice ceased. The duck parted the reeds.

There sat a large goose. Her head and neck were black, and she had a white patch on both of her cheeks. In a circle around her, sitting on water-lily pads, were eight very small frogs who, just as the duck stepped forward, jumped one by one into the pond.

"Tell me," asked the duck with a broad smile, "are you by any chance a relative of the goose that laid the golden eggs?"

The goose looked thoughtful. "No, I don't believe so," she replied. "I don't recall anyone in my family doing such a thing."

"Well," said the duck heartily, "that doesn't matter at all. There's more to life than golden eggs, isn't there?" And before the goose could reply, he hurried on. "But I didn't come here to discuss legends. You interest me. I think you and I could make a great team. I'm a manager, you see. You may have heard about me. I put on theatrical shows, and many an animal has gone on to fame and fortune as a result of my efforts. Now, about you. If you could tell me a story or two, samples, so to speak, I can judge whether you're ready for the stage."

The goose looked puzzled. "I'm not really interested in the stage," she said, "but thank you for considering me."

Even better, thought the duck. A creature without ambition will be no trouble at all!

"Let me persuade you," said the duck with what he hoped was a winning smile. "I can see you love to tell stories. I could tell by the feeling in your voice. Why not share those stories with a larger audience, not just frogs?"

"I like frogs," the goose protested mildly.

"Oh—of course!" cried the duck. "We all like frogs! But what about your career?"

"I don't have such a thing," said the goose.

"It just so happens I'm a critic, too," said the duck hastily. "I could help you with your stories—make them more appealing, more *theat-*

rical, so to speak. You know what I mean?" And the duck laughed extravagantly. "Don't be shy," he begged. "Do tell me a story!"

The goose cast a glance at the sky. It would not be long before sunset, and she was rather tired. But she was obliging, and she did love to tell stories.

"All right," she said at last. "I don't mind passing the time of day with you. But I'm quite sure I wouldn't like the stage."

"We'll see," said the duck, settling down among the reeds, secretly sure he could convince her later on.

"Do you know the story of the Little Swineherd?" asked the goose.

"Never heard of it," said the duck.

"A long time ago . . ." the goose began.

"How long?" interrupted the duck.

"Oh, years and years. . . ."

"Before there were cars?"

"Oh, yes," replied the goose. "Most of the stories I know happened before there were cars."

The duck was annoyed to see that the frogs were climbing back on their lily pads to listen. Somewhat impatiently, he said, "Go on, go on!"

"In that time long ago, in a small valley hidden from the world, was a cottage, an old barn, a small chicken coop, and a pigsty. In the cottage lived an elderly couple, Mr. and Mrs. Gudge, and a boy who

was the swineherd. There were a few laying hens in the coop, a horse in the barn, and many, many pigs in the sty."

"What was the boy's name?" asked the duck.

"The boy was an orphan and wasn't sure of his name. But later on, as you will see, he named himself, as orphans often do," explained the goose.

"But—" the duck began.

"Perhaps you'd better just listen," said the goose with a touch of sternness.

"Of course!" said the duck. "Proceed!"

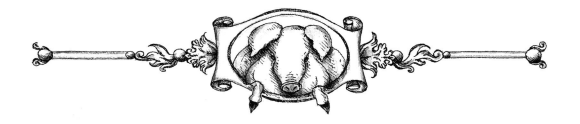

The Little Swineherd

He lives with pigs!" the children cried every morning on their way to school just as they were passing the pigsty where the little swineherd was emptying a bucket of slops into a trough. And every morning, at the farthest edge of the meadow where the woods began, the children turned back and waved at the little swineherd and burst into shouts of laughter, as though they had thought of still other comical things about him.

It was hard to be laughed at for simply doing what he had to do, and simply being what he was. But the little swineherd never answered them. He never looked up from his work until the last lingering note

of their cries had melted in the still morning air as icicles melt in the sunlight.

The pigs guzzled in the trough. They snorted and grunted and squealed. But the little swineherd was so accustomed to their noise, he hardly heard it. He was so used to the stench of the slops and the pigs and the mud, he hardly smelled it. He was so used to taking care of the pigs in any kind of weather—the bitter cold of winter, the heat of summer, the sharp windy days of spring and fall—that shivering or sweating was all the same to him. When it rained, he put on an old cap and an old jacket that had belonged to someone else, and though he was always soaked through, he didn't notice that either.

Only thunder and lightning made him look up at the sky, then down, across the meadow, to the woods beyond which he had not been. As the thunder rolled through the valley like a giant hoop and as the lightning mottled the dark sky, he would think of mysterious things he could hardly put words to—round, slowly turning things like the moon or the sun; long, narrow things like paths leading to faraway places, or streams winding through forests, becoming rivers, racing over cliffs, and spreading out into vast lakes; and blurred, small things like the faces of a distant crowd of people whose features he could not make out, but whose voices he strained to hear through the claps of thunder and the crackle of lightning. Dreaming these things, he often breathed two words to himself: *the world*.

After the pigs were fed and quiet, sinking their sticklike legs into the mud and twitching their ears and curly tails as they looked for a place to sleep, the little swineherd thought about Mr. and Mrs. Gudge, the elderly couple in whose cottage he had a bed but little else. Every day, Mrs. Gudge said to him, "If it hadn't been for us, who knows what would have become of you?" And Mr. Gudge said, "Count the day we found you as the luckiest day of your life!"

Why was that? he wondered. And if that *was* the luckiest day of his life, what on earth would the rest of his days be like?

The cottage was a good distance from the sty, but the little swineherd could see Mr. and Mrs. Gudge through the window, as busy with eating as the pigs. In the morning, they ate thick porridge, then they napped. At dinner, in the middle of the day, they ate a meat pie and then a fruit pie. And they napped again. In the early evening, before the light faded, they drank cups of tea, and in bowls slowly stirred round and round three boiled eggs each.

"You are much too young for such food," Mrs. Gudge said once when she saw him steal a glance at the soft yellow yolks of the eggs, which she always saved for last, and she handed him the hard loaf of bread and wedge of crumbly cheese that were all he was ever given.

In the summer, he found red berries beneath the tall grass in the meadow, so sweet to taste they made him shiver. Sometimes he picked up a windfall from beneath an apple tree that had gone wild and crooked from neglect. He polished the hard little apple on his ragged jacket, and when he bit into it, his lips drew back at its bitterness.

He filled a mug from the pump at the back of the cottage, but in late summer, the well was often low. Sometimes only gray sow bugs fell out of the pump's spout. Then he had to walk to the stream at the base of the meadow to get a drink of water.

"You're much too old to depend on us for water," said Mrs. Gudge. "You've got strong legs of your own and can go to the stream." And then she would take a dipper and fill it for herself from the pail of water Mr. Gudge had stored away.

At nightfall, the little swineherd went to his bed in a lean-to at the back of the cottage. His bed was a board laid across two sawhorses. His mattress was an old horse blanket. His covering was a heap of ancient clothes that would keep his legs warm, or his shoulders, but never both. In the winter, he froze, and in the summer, he burned. Through a crack in the wall he often watched the glimmering yellow glow of the kerosene light on the table, and heard Mr. and Mrs. Gudge speak of the profits they expected from the sale of the pigs. As the drone of their voices went on into the deepest part of the night, the lamp's glow seemed as bright as that of the sun, and in it the little swineherd imagined he saw the schoolchildren coming toward him, smiling, their hands held out, full of apples and eggs and loaves of fresh bread.

Once in a while, Mr. and Mrs. Gudge went to bed as early as he did. Then, for company, he had only the sound of the feet of chipmunks scrabbling on the roof, and he was reminded of how a soft early-spring rain started up, with just such a gentle tapping.

Once, on his way to the sty, he came across a small snake sunning itself, and he walked around it carefully so it would stay where it was and he could think about it while he fed the pigs. He liked to know animals were nearby—not chickens and pigs so much, but animals that went their own way. He especially liked the sharp, lively cries of the blue jays and the great wild honking of the geese when they flew south at the end of the summer. He liked, too, the fish he saw darting through the stream—geese and fish, on their way somewhere else, out of the valley.

Sometimes he went to stare at the old workhorse in the barn, which stood silently, looking neither to the right nor to the left but straight ahead at the barn siding. Even when the horse grazed, it appeared to be looking at nothing as it tossed up a mouthful of grass and chomped away. The horse drew the wagon that took Mr. and Mrs. Gudge to a town far from the cottage where they bought supplies and sold the pigs. The little swineherd did not remember the town, although Mr. Gudge had once remarked that that was where they had found him.

There was very little talk between the little swineherd and Mr. and Mrs. Gudge. When they spoke to him, they reminded him of the horse. They stared neither to the right nor to the left; their glance went just beyond him, over his head.

They were not especially cruel to him. They were not kind. The little swineherd did not hate them—they were just there, like a special kind of bleak weather that would not go away. Yet, now and then, a powerful longing arose in him. If only they would speak to him of things other than the pigs, or the well, or whether he was too young or too old for this or for that!

But Mr. Gudge, who was short and plump, and Mrs. Gudge, who was tall and plump, hardly spoke to each other, unless it was about the pigs or dinner, and they never smiled, and their voices were always the same, like straight lines drawn in the dust. The little swineherd wondered if they would ever like to fly from the valley like the geese.

They always called the little swineherd *you*. But he believed he had a name—if he could find it. It was hidden somewhere, like an apple in tall grass, but he knew it would not be bitter. Names swam through his mind as the fish swam through the stream, names he had heard the schoolchildren call each other—Harry and Keith and Charles and Peter and Luke and Lawrence and Tom and Adam and Edward. Edward! That was the name he always returned to in his thoughts. *Edward,* he often said aloud as he fed the pigs. Perhaps he was an Edward, too.

He did live with pigs, and he didn't like them very much. The young ones made him smile, but the old ones scared him when they rushed toward the slop bucket, like barrels with red eyes. If pigs could talk, he guessed, they wouldn't have anything to say unless it was about food—and a word or two about mud. Food and mud and scratching their bristly backs against the fence posts, that's all that ever concerned them. Yet, when it came time for Mr. and Mrs. Gudge to take them to market, he felt sorry for them. He felt a sinking sensation in his belly when the old horse was brought out of the barn and harnessed, and when the pigs were sorted out and the ones to be sold were loaded onto the back of the wagon. He would never see them again, not those pigs. They were not going anywhere they wanted to go, not like the geese whose flight the little swineherd imitated in the meadow when he was sure no one was watching, flapping his arms and jumping and honking.

But that day always came, the day the pigs were sorted out, and the little pigs without their mothers and the mothers without their little pigs squealed all day and all night.

On such a day, after a year in which the little swineherd had never seen so many pigs born in the sty, Mr. and Mrs. Gudge dressed in their town clothes; then Mrs. Gudge said something to the little swineherd she had never said before.

"After we have left," she said, looking just over his head at the cottage, "you may go to the chicken coop and take two eggs for your dinner."

"And," said Mr. Gudge, "you may make yourself a cup of my China tea—that is, if you can guess how."

The little swineherd continued to gaze down the road, long after the

wagon, the pigs, and Mr. and Mrs. Gudge had disappeared. What had they meant? Was he old enough now? For eggs and tea?

In the coop he found five eggs. He left three for Mr. and Mrs. Gudge. In a tin box on a cupboard shelf he found the tea. He boiled water for the tea in the kettle on the stove over the remains of the morning's fire, and he boiled the eggs, too. Then he sat down to the best dinner he had ever had—although the eggs had cooked too long. He sighed. What a fine thing it was to eat well and enough! Yet he was uneasy.

That afternoon there was the most violent storm he had ever experienced. The sky turned black as a night without stars; the thunder seemed to come, not from above, but from the deepest, darkest, most unknown part of the earth, and the lightning struck the ground with such force, the little swineherd expected that the valley would be shattered like a dropped plate.

After, there was a pale blue sky, no wind at all, a wet fresh silence. In the thunder's last parting echo, the little swineherd imagined he heard words: *They may never come back.* Or had he said them himself?

He lit the kerosene lamp himself that night, remembering how Mrs. Gudge had done it, and he placed the lamp in the cottage window in case the Gudges returned. He looked at the meat pies that lined the cupboard shelves but dared not take a piece of one. Instead, he ate the hard bread he was used to, and a piece of the crumbly cheese. Then he settled down to wait, close to the door.

No one came. The lamp glowed, as always. Across the roof the chipmunks tapped like raindrops. A night bird called out as it flew through the valley. The moon, pale as though washed by the storm, rose and set. A hen clucked dreamily as dawn cast its first light across the meadow. The little swineherd was alone for the first morning of his life.

"Edward," he said, to comfort himself. "Go and feed the hens and the pigs." But his heart felt like a stone. The cottage was damp, the earth floor was cold, the fire in the stove had gone out.

Gradually, as the sun rose in the sky, the little swineherd began to move about the cottage. He saw many things he had never seen before. He wondered how he could have lived all his life in such a small place and noticed so little. Clocks and chests, jam and jelly jars, honeypots, shelves of cups and bowls and pitchers. He lifted the lid of a trunk. Inside were rusty tools without handles and broken handles without tools. In fact, everything was broken or dented or cracked or rusty or bent. Except for the food supply. He was astonished to find so many sacks of potatoes, such a huge slab of smoked meat, so many jars of pickles and jellies, so many loaves of bread and rounds of cheese, and pies and porridge and salt and sugar.

The pigs were complaining from the sty, and the hens were clucking in the coop. The little swineherd peered through the window. It was not a usual day. For here he was, inside, and the schoolchildren were passing on their way to school. He saw them look up toward the sty, and speak to each other, and look again. It made him feel strange to *see* them thinking about him, talking about him. The sun had melted away the morning mist, and the valley lay in a buttery light.

The little swineherd fed the hens from a sack of grain. He found a bucket of slops outside the lean-to where Mrs. Gudge must have left it, and took it to the sty. Only a few pigs pressed against the railing, their little restless eyes fixed on the bucket. Five piglets, too small for market, lay spread out like the pink fingers of a fat hand, their snouts pressed against the teats of their big mud-covered mother. A breeze came up, and the meadow grass rustled. The little swineherd did not miss Mr. and Mrs. Gudge, but he missed something. He stood outside the sty and looked up the road, then down the road. He went to lean against the trunk of the old apple tree. He observed the ants that crawled over and around a fallen branch brought down by yesterday's storm. He went to the banks of the stream. Three silver fish swam by. A field mouse ran across a stick. The little swineherd was lonely.

He waited all afternoon, he wasn't sure for what. Only an old farmer passed, walking behind a cranky-looking mule, and, later on, the children on their way home. But they were quiet, as always at the end of the day, and did not look up but dreamily watched their own feet as they moved down the road.

Evening came. The little swineherd lit the lamp. What had happened to Mr. and Mrs. Gudge? Had the thunder and lightning killed them? Had the wagon tipped over a ditch and fallen on them? Had a robber made off with the pigs and left the old man and the old woman dead?

On the third morning of his being alone, the little swineherd was amazed to look up and see the head of the old horse pressing up against the window, looking in at him. He ran out of the cottage. The horse whinnied. There was dried foam around his mouth, and he was as muddy as the old sow after a good roll.

"What happened?" asked the little swineherd. The horse tossed his head, then nodded up and down. The little swineherd started off toward the barn, and the horse followed. He brushed the horse's coat with a brush so large he could barely keep hold of it, and he gave him oats. Then he led him to the meadow. "Now this meadow is yours," he said. The horse began to graze.

The little swineherd felt less alone. He put twigs and sticks in the stove in the cottage, and he struck a spark off a flint and the fire began. He put the kettle on for tea.

As the days passed, the little swineherd discovered that the laughter of the schoolchildren no longer troubled him. And as it ceased to trouble him, they seemed to laugh less. In fact, the little swineherd was glad that they passed him in the morning as he took care of the pigs. He would have missed them if they'd gone to school a different way. He learned which name belonged to which boy and girl. In the afternoon, he watched them from the cottage window, and was pleased, one day, when the girl called Flora waved, and the boy called Luke smiled at him.

The little swineherd ate eggs every day for his dinner. He kept the fire going in the stove, learning how to stoke it so it would burn all night and in the morning still be going.

He gave all the hard loaves of bread and the crumbly cheese to the pigs.

Would he be alone in the valley for the rest of his life? The horse and he spent many hours in the meadow. The horse followed the little swineherd willingly, it seemed, and he neighed happily in the morning when he was let out of the barn. At least, the little swineherd thought he was happy.

One rainy morning, the little swineherd put on the old jacket, and it ripped right down the middle. He put on his old boots, and he couldn't lace them. He looked at the cupboard shelves and saw he'd eaten all the meat pies and most of the fruit pies and most of the jelly and jam and some of the pickles. There was other food, but he didn't know how to cook it. The pigs were getting less and less to eat; there was hardly enough left over to feed them. And the kerosene was getting so low, the little swineherd lit the lamp only when there was no moonlight.

He realized he would have to do something, or else terrible hard times would be coming. But whatever could he do? He'd not been to the towns outside the valley. He didn't know the farmers who lived in the valley. He knew no one, unless he counted Flora and Luke and the horse.

"Edward," he said to himself loudly. "You will have to leave the cottage and the valley and go and find a home elsewhere."

Then he thought of the pigs and the chickens and the horse. He couldn't leave them alone to starve. But if he stayed, he would starve himself!

What if he took the animals with him? Some farmer would surely be glad to get such a fine sow and her piglets, such large hens, and a workhorse that could pull a wagon. It's true that the old horse sagged somewhat in the middle, but he was an agreeable animal.

But how?

The horse would follow him, but not the pigs or the chickens. The little swineherd thought and thought, and while he thought, he paced about the cottage and restlessly opened one trunk, then another. He had decided he would have to carry the pigs and chickens out of the valley two by two, when his glance fell upon an old hand net in the biggest trunk. He remembered how Mr. Gudge had, now and then, tried to scoop a fish out of the stream with it. A net!

He found a ball of twine and, with the aid of a paring knife, he cut and tied and braided and wove it until he had an oddly shaped net with holes of different sizes that covered nearly the whole floor of the cottage. He hoped the holes were not so large that the animals could slip out from them and run away, or so small that they would choke if they moved.

He put the last of the bread and one jar of jam and a handful of grain and a wedge of yellow cheese into an old sack. Then he made sure the fire was out.

Early the next morning, long before the children passed on their way to school, the little swineherd gathered together the pigs and the chickens and the horse. "My boots are too tight," he told them, shivering a bit in the early-morning chill, "and I've gotten too big for the old jacket, and there isn't enough to feed you." The chickens scratched in the ground, the pigs looked around for the slop bucket, and the old horse stood patiently, nodding his head.

Then the little swineherd began to set the pigs and the chickens into the net like raisins in a pudding. At first the animals were so surprised by this turn of events that they were silent. The little swineherd gathered up the ends of the net, clicked his tongue at the horse, and set off down the road leading out of the valley.

At once there was a horrible racket as the pigs plunged in one direction and the hens tried to fly in all directions. The horse, frightened by all the noise, reared up and whinnied. The net had turned into a wheel of roaring angry pigs and squawking outraged hens. The little swineherd let go of the net and sat down in the ditch and covered his face with his hands.

He wished the thunder and lightning would come and take him away. He wished the stream would flood its banks and carry him off to the places where the fishes went. He wished the birds would make a great platform of their wings and fly him over the hills.

"Going somewhere?" inquired a voice.

The little swineherd took his hands away from his face. An old man was standing on the other side of the road, looking at him with an obliging smile. He had a beard, a woolen cap pulled down over his head, and, most surprising, one blue eye and one brown eye. There

was a large, full pack on his back, and in his hand he held a rope, and attached to the rope was a small nanny goat busy munching the grass that grew at the edge of the road.

The horse was grazing peacefully in the meadow. The pigs and chickens, exhausted by their exertions, were lying about in the dust, grunting and clucking despairingly, their heads still poking up through the openings of the net.

"Seeing is not always believing," observed the old man. "I wonder what you have in mind?"

"There isn't much more I can eat," said the little swineherd. "I had to find a new place for all of us." He stopped speaking, hoping he'd explained enough. The old man nodded.

"Is that your cottage?" he asked.

"I live in it," replied the little swineherd.

"Let us extract the pigs and chickens from your net. They can then recover their natural optimism in the sty and the hen yard. Then we'll think about what's to be done."

With the old man's help, the little swineherd returned the animals to where they belonged. Then the old man drove a large stick into the ground and tied the goat's rope around it. "Now let's see the cottage," he said.

He looked all around, at the stove, at the board in the lean-to where the little swineherd had continued to sleep, at the stove, at the cupboard, at the sacks of potatoes.

"There's plenty to eat," he said at last. "It only needs cooking. I see you have a pump out there, so that's all right. This place could certainly use some work. I would say it's the gloomiest place I've seen in some time."

"I never thought about it," said the little swineherd. "Although I've always liked it better outside in the meadow."

"I should think so," said the old man.

"Are you from the town?" asked the little swineherd timidly. He was not accustomed to asking questions.

"I'm from a good many towns," answered the old man. "And my name is Ira Winks, and my goat and I have been on the road for many years. It's been my intention to reach the West. But it has certainly taken a long time since I started in that direction over thirty years ago. I guess you must live here alone, for if you had a mother or a father or even a wicked stepfather, you wouldn't have been out there on the road performing such pranks with your domestic animals. If you'll just go and fetch a pail of water, I'll start a pot of soup."

The little swineherd was astonished by all the words that had been spoken to him. He was glad to go and get the water from the pump so that he could think over what had been said.

When he returned, the old man had a fire going in the stove and he was peeling potatoes.

"What's your name?" asked Ira Winks.

"Edward," replied the little swineherd at once, determined from that moment on to be known by no other name.

"Well, Edward, do you have a last name?"

"I don't believe so," said Edward. "Perhaps I did once. Are you going to stay here for a while?"

"I think I will," said Ira. "The West has waited this long for me to get there. It can wait a bit longer. What nice turnips! I'll just add them to the pot."

After they had eaten, Ira Winks asked, "How did you come by this place, and have you always lived here alone?"

Edward took a while to answer. He was not used to speaking of himself. Also, he didn't know how his life had begun.

"I'm not sure how I got here," he began. "But I've been here as long as I can think back. Mr. and Mrs. Gudge—they're the people who lived here until they took the pigs to market—said it was the luckiest day of my life when they found me. Then, a while back, they harnessed the horse and took the pigs in the wagon to market. The horse came back alone and looked through the window at me. And that's all I know."

"That's quite a few mysteries," said Ira. "Perhaps you were left on their doorstep when you were an infant? Perhaps you are under a spell? Or a great bird left you in a saucer? Or were you washed up on the beach by a wave? You don't have a mysterious locket around your neck, do you? No, I didn't think so. I mean to say—the main thing is you're here now. And when you grow up, you can set out to discover the secret of your birth, if you want to, that is."

Edward was intoxicated by Ira Winks's speech. No one had ever spoken to him at such length and in such a way. Although he'd hardly heard what the old man said except when he talked about growing up. Until that moment, he'd thought—if he thought about it at all—that he would be a little swineherd all his life.

"But what could have happened to Mr. and Mrs. Gudge?" he wondered.

"Tomorrow I will go to town," said Ira, "and see what I can find out." He looked around the cottage.

"What a terrible sad place this is," he remarked again. "We must get at it. Is that where you sleep? In that nasty little lean-to?"

"It's my bed," said Edward.

"I say to the Gudges, good riddance," said Ira Winks. "They didn't treat you kindly, I can see that. The question is, how are we to get what we need so we can put this place to rights?"

Edward had never thought of the cottage as being to rights or to wrongs. All he knew of comfort was the way his dinners had improved since the disappearance of the old couple.

"I have it!" said Ira Winks, snapping his fingers.

"Your eyes are different colors," said Edward, who had been staring at him.

"Yes, that's been noticed," said the old man. "You'll get used to it."

"It's very nice," said Edward, and was pleased with himself. He couldn't ever remember saying such a thing before. "Do you see different things with each eye?"

"Only now and then," said the old man, laughing. Edward laughed, too, just for the pleasure of it. "About my plan . . . what we must do is hold a barn sale, and when I go to town tomorrow, I'll see to it that everyone hears of it. We'll trade and we'll take coins, too. Whatever we can get." He began to walk about the room, picking up things and setting them down. Then he flung open the lid of a trunk. "Just as I thought," he said. "Old trunks are always filled with things that aren't useful but that everyone wants! Look at that old knife handle! What a thing of beauty! And that clock! For that we should be able to get enough whitewash to make this whole cottage as fresh as a daisy, and for the dented pots, enough nails to lay down a floor. . . ." And so the old man went on until he seemed to have named everything in the cottage.

"I think we should keep the chickens, don't you?" he asked Edward. "And though the horse eats a good deal, he'll come in handy when we trade the pigs for a plow. That's all right with you, isn't it?"

Edward could hardly imagine life without pigs.

"I've always lived with pigs," he said, remembering how the children used to shout at him. It seemed so long ago.

"Well, Edward," said Ira Winks, "you must decide, for I won't put them up for trade or sale without your say-so."

"But they're not really mine," said Edward, looking around the cottage at the trunks and chests and the clock and the kerosene lamp. "There's nothing here that's mine."

"It's all been left you," said the old man. "And if the Gudges ever return, they'll find everything better than they left it."

"But the pigs will be gone."

"We will put aside what profit we make to pay the Gudges."

"The thunder said they might never come back," said Edward. "At least, I thought that's what it said."

"You can't believe everything you hear," said Ira Winks.

"Will people really come to buy and trade?"

"You'll see!" promised Ira. "After I spread the word around, they'll turn up in droves!"

"Then spread the word around about the pigs, too," said Edward.

Ira Winks went to feed the nanny goat. Edward sat next to the stove in a trance. Eating such a lot of soup had made him sleepy, but the thought of the changes in his life kept him awake.

The old man started off for town before the sun was up. He left the little goat tethered near the cottage door, and Edward was glad she was there because he was sure the old man would come back for her.

And he did return that afternoon, walking briskly down the road and full of news.

"We'll hold the great barn sale in two days," he said, "which will give us time to clear out the barn as well as the cottage. I'm sure there's many a rag of a thing, or fragment or segment or bit of a thing in the barn that will tempt our customers."

He stroked the goat's head. "Good Nanny," he said.

Edward waited eagerly, then asked, "And *them*?"

"Them," repeated Ira. "I heard they sold the pigs at an unheard-of profit, and that they bought themselves steamer trunks. Then Mr. Gudge announced they were leaving to see the world, and Mrs. Gudge wrapped a fur piece around her throat, and Mr. Gudge lit up a long cigar, and they departed and have not been seen or heard of since. Of course, the world is round, so they might indeed come back, but not for a very long time."

"I wonder what a long time is," said Edward.

"So long you won't remember the color of their eyes."

Edward had never noticed the color of the Gudges' eyes, but he didn't mention that.

"We have work to do," Ira Winks said. "Now, here's how we must do it."

Edward did exactly as Ira said, and soon the slope in front of the cottage was covered with surprising objects. There were coffee grinders and small braided rugs, little chipped plates, horseshoes and rusty saws, empty barrels and green glass bottles, old shoes and an inkwell, bits and bridles and lengths of harness, the runners of an old sled, lanterns and lamps and ladles, a pair of old boots, in one of which lived a mouse—"We won't sell the mouse," said Ira, "so take him out to the meadow and let him go"—and a feather duster with only two feathers left, and a black saddle, and a washtub with a hole in the bottom, and a pillow that smelled of pine needles, a shaving mug with a picture of a moose on it, a wheelbarrow without a wheel, and such a multitude of torn and bent and rusted and twisted and cracked and dented and moldy things that Edward could hardly believe his eyes!

"But who will want all this?" he asked.

"Everyone!" cried Ira Winks. "There's nothing more satisfying to people than to get a bit of rusted wire for a penny or two."

Ira had set aside a few articles he thought they might need themselves—a hoe, two quilts that he'd found stuffed in a barrel, and the old kettle, which he polished up with a rag until it gleamed.

Edward cleaned out the sty, too, as much as he could. "I'm not a swineherd now," he said to the old sow. She grunted and wallowed and paid no attention.

The next morning, the schoolchildren came to a halt in front of the cottage, where Ira Winks was putting down a three-legged table with a cracked top. The children looked at all the things, then at one another, then they burst into wild shouts of laughter.

"A mountain of rubbish!" cried one of the boys.

"A hill of trash!" shouted one of the girls.

"A slope of slop!" howled the biggest boy.

But Flora stepped out from the group and said politely to Edward, "Are these things for sale or for trade?" He was too shy to answer, but Ira Winks spoke right up, saying, "Both. Every one of these fine treasures is up for sale or for trade."

"How much are the blue chipped bowls?" asked Flora.

"Each a penny," said the old man with a smile. Flora dug into the pocket of her coat and produced a penny and held it out, and Ira handed her a bowl. The children gathered around to look at it, then they waved at Ira and Edward and went along on their way to school.

"There!" exclaimed Ira Winks. "You see? That's a good omen. You just wait!"

By suppertime, there wasn't a scrap of anything left in front of the cottage. In fact, Edward was surprised the cottage itself was still there. The road had been filled with people all day long, coming or going, buying or trading, arguing or agreeing.

Ira Winks poured out two glasses of goat's milk. "We must drink a toast to our luck," he said. "And now we can please ourselves!" They drank the goat's milk, and then they looked over what they'd gotten. There were buckets of lime and whiting to make whitewash, a big hammer, bags of nails of all sizes, an awl, an adze, a clamp, files, a pitchfork, a roast turkey, a barrel of apples, three pairs of knitted wool socks, a bolt of dark wool cloth, a nearly new pot, seven forks, a saw, and, best of all, a nearly new plow that a farmer had given in exchange for the pigs. There were a few other odd bits—similar to what they'd been traded for—but there was one brand-new object, a large mirror, framed in wood with two carved wooden birds at the top.

"Take a look at yourself," offered Ira, holding out the mirror.

The little swineherd peered at the glass, then jumped back with a frightened cry.

"Oh, now, a wash will do wonders for you, Edward," Ira said soothingly. "You'll see what a fine face you have! I can already see it right through the mud!"

But Edward was saddened by his image in the mirror. He looked out the window at the moonlight on the meadow. No wonder the children made fun of him! He looked toward the empty sty. The pigs were all gone. Who was he now that he was no longer a swineherd?

"Edward" didn't belong to *him*. It was just a name he'd picked out that belonged to someone else. He felt two tears drop down his cheeks.

Then he went out to the barn and stood in the dark, listening to the old horse breathing quietly, smelling the barn smells. The horse whinnied softly. Edward stroked his neck. He almost wished he was walking to the sty of a morning, carrying a bucket of slops, with the old couple eating their porridge in the dirty, gloomy old cottage, and the children about to pass him and cry that he lived with pigs!

Where on earth did anything come from? And where was everything going?

"Ira Winks? Where did you come from and where are you going?" he asked when he got back to the cottage.

"I see the tracks of two tears on your cheeks," said Ira. He was cutting up the bolt of dark cloth with a pair of scissors.

"Won't you tell me?" asked Edward.

"I started in the south," began the old man. "Then I traveled north, and then I went east. I decided that what I wanted might be in the west, and I was starting that way thirty years ago when I stopped to help a farmer plant his corn. I always seemed to be stopping for one reason or another, I've done all kinds of work and I'm handy, but my feet get itchy and I start moving on, so all I've got to show for my life is in my pack and that old nanny goat out there that I got for sawing up a winter's supply of stove wood. I've lived where it pleased me, and I've moved on when it pleased me. I suppose you could say I was a drifter, like the milkweed down in the meadow."

"Then you might move on from here any minute?" asked Edward.

The old man began to pin the cloth. Then he took a needle from his jacket and threaded it.

"I'm making you a new winter jacket," he said, stitching away at the cloth. "Tomorrow, I'm going back to town. We must have soap and candles, and you must have new boots and mittens. I smell winter. I heard the geese flying south today."

"And will you go, too, when the geese have all gone?"

"No, I won't go then. I've got a new plan. We can sell eggs and the cheese I know how to make from Nanny's milk. We'll put up a nice little stand in front of the cottage. We'll have all winter to make this cottage fine. And you must go to school."

"School!" cried Edward. "But I can't even read!"

"That's why," said Ira Winks. "So that you'll learn." He stitched faster and faster, and the needle seemed to fly in and out, looping and straightening and pulling the pieces of cloth together.

"And after that?" asked Edward.

"The spring will come and we'll plant a vegetable garden and I'll prune the apple tree in the meadow."

"Can't you teach me to read?" asked Edward.

"I only know a few letters," said the old man with a touch of regret. "I can tell time and I can count. But I can't teach you to read."

"I can't think why I *should* learn to read," said Edward.

"How will you leave the valley if you can't even read a road sign?" asked Ira Winks. "Why, I've gone hundreds of miles out of my way just because I couldn't read a simple sign, and gotten myself into some pickles, too! And gone where I had no intention of going, and missed the places where I really wanted to go. And now I've got your new jacket started. It's time to have some roast turkey and tea. We've a lot to do tomorrow."

In less than a week, Ira Winks had whitewashed the stone walls of the cottage, and put down a floor of wood, and washed the old quilts he'd found, and polished the stove, and fixed all the broken furniture, and made Edward a new bed. Where everything had once been dark and dank, everything became light and dry and warm. Edward liked the sound his new boots made on the new floor, and he wore the jacket even though it was not really cold yet.

They took down the sty and cut up the wood for winter. And they found enough planks in the barn to build a small stand. Ira painted it bright yellow with paint he had bought in the town. Then they made a stall for the nanny goat in the barn so that, when it got too cold, she'd have a place to shelter.

"We must have a sign," said Ira one day after they'd finished the stand. "There's our first true problem. The sign must tell people what we have to sell. I might manage to spell 'eggs,' but 'cheese,' never! Of course, I could take some of the pennies we got during our great sale and hire someone in town to make a sign. But I'd rather not. We'll need our money for other things."

Edward shook his head. "I don't see what we can do," he said. "Couldn't we just tell all the farmers and all the townspeople what we have to sell?"

"We must have a sign," insisted Ira. Then he saw the children coming down the road on their way home. "You can ask the girl who bought the blue bowl," suggested the old man.

"Oh, I can't!" exclaimed Edward. "They'll laugh at me! They'll know I can't read or write."

"But you can't," said the old man in his kindly way. "And neither can I."

Edward looked at Ira's blue eye and his brown eye. He looked around the cottage that was now so neat and clean and cheerful. He looked at the horse in the meadow and the nanny goat on her tether. A hen clucked loudly in the hen yard. The children were coming closer and closer.

"Go ahead," urged the old man.

Edward put on his new jacket and walked toward the children. When they saw him, the boys began to laugh and the girls began to smile. "Flora?" he asked.

She came right up to him. "Go ahead," she said to the others. "I'll catch up."

"We can't read or write," he said, "and we must have a sign so that people will know we can sell them eggs and goat cheese."

Flora opened a notebook and wrote out the letters on a sheet of paper, then she handed it to Edward.

"Thank you," he said. He couldn't remember ever saying that before in his life.

"You're welcome," she said. "What happened to all those pigs?"

"We traded them for a plow."

"You and your grandfather?"

Edward hesitated. He would have liked to say yes. "He's not really my grandfather," he said.

"Will you ever come to school?" she asked.

With a sudden rush of gladness, Edward said, "Soon."

He took the sheet of paper to Ira, and Ira copied out the letters on a board with yellow paint. Then he nailed the sign to the stand. "I hope I've got it right side up," he said.

How changed everything was in Edward's life! By the time the first snow fell, farmers and their wives came regularly to the little stand to buy goat cheese, and the townspeople drove out in their buggies to buy fresh eggs. More and more glass jars of pennies lined the cottage shelves, and the cottage itself was snug and weathertight. The fire in the stove was always burning. The barn glistened in the clear winter sunlight with its new coat of paint. There was a rooster in the hen yard, and a kitten named Jennie who purred all night at the foot of Edward's bed. Edward was warm at night, and warm in the morning. He had mittens to wear when he went out to bring in wood for the stove, or feed the horse, or wrap up the cheese for the customers.

"The time has come for you to begin school," said Ira Winks one morning.

Edward's heart beat fast.

"I'm scared," he said.

"I should think so," said Ira. "But that will wear off."

"When?" asked Edward.

"After the first five minutes of the second morning," replied Ira. "Now I think I'll trim your hair." And he took a pair of scissors from his old pack.

"Why do that?" asked Edward.

"So that you'll look more even. Then you'll feel more even."

Afterward, Edward looked at his cut hair. It was dark, and silky as feathers. He looked at himself in the framed mirror with the two wooden birds at the top. That was the little swineherd with his hair evened up, he thought. An old sadness rose in him like a small spring bubbling up.

"I don't know who I look like," he said.

"Like yourself," said the old man.

The next morning, Ira made two sandwiches for Edward's lunch, and he put the sandwiches and an apple in a bag. "It's time," he said. Jennie purred at the door. Edward looked longingly around the warm cottage, then at the kettle on the stove. "Some changes are better than others," he said. Ira took his hand, and they set off down the road toward the school.

And when they rounded the edge of the woods, there was the whole countryside that lay beyond the valley. The little stream became a river; there were great fields dotted with farms and barns and silos.

Far ahead of them, Edward saw the schoolchildren walking along and swinging their schoolbags. And ahead of the children, Edward saw a church steeple, and the roofs and chimneys of a town.

"Let's go home," he suggested to Ira Winks.

"You know everything at home," replied Ira.

"Do I have to learn everything there is?" he asked.

"No," answered Ira, "just some of what there is."

Edward felt somewhat comforted.

A bell rang.

Edward stopped in his tracks.

"Come along," said Ira firmly. "That is the school bell."

Edward looked at the small square building with the long windows and the little belfry where the bell hung. All the children he recognized, as well as some children he had never seen, were crowded up to the windows looking out at Ira and Edward.

He remembered the times when nothing changed. He remembered how Mrs. Gudge used to tell him what day was the luckiest day of his life. What was going to happen next?

A woman came to the door. A silvery braid coiled around her head. She smiled. "Here's a new face," she said. "You're just in time!"

"For what?" asked Edward uneasily.

"Peninsulas, islands, nesses, necks, aits, islets, continents, and other landmasses," she replied.

Edward clutched Ira's hand.

"That's enough, isn't it?" he asked Ira.

"That's a beginning," said Ira. "I'll see you in the afternoon. We'll all be waiting for you to come home." He withdrew his hand and patted Edward's shoulder and, without another word, turned and went back down the road toward the cottage.

The woman reached out and took Edward's hand. "I'm the teacher," she said. "My name is Mrs. Elsa Henry. There is a desk for you, and a hook where you can hang up your fine jacket. Wipe your boots on the mat, and, when you go in, put your lunch on the shelf."

As soon as Edward had walked into the classroom, a boy made soft pig sounds. "Oink! Oink!" Some of the children giggled and some only smiled. But Luke and Flora waved at Edward.

"Tell me your name," said Mrs. Henry, "and I will write it on the blackboard."

"Edward Winks," said Edward, surprised to hear his voice so clear and loud.

Some of the children clapped their hands, and Edward didn't know whether they were making fun of him or being friendly. He decided to say everything that was on his mind and get it over with right now.

"I can't read or write," he said. "And I don't know numbers neither."

"You've come to the right place," said Mrs. Henry. "You're a *tabula rasa*—that means a clean slate in Latin, children. And that's how every-thing begins."

For a long time, school was hard for Edward. Some of the children continued to tease him, but others grew friendly. By the spring, he had learned letters and quite a few words, and one afternoon when the daylight had begun to lengthen and the snow had thawed and the earth had grown warmer, Edward brought home a book and read a few of its pages to Ira.

"This is a lucky day in my life," said Ira.

Edward was happy.

He learned to do sums, too, although he could never add up all the pennies in the jars as quickly as Ira Winks could.

When the right time came, Ira plowed up the land where once the pigsty had stood. He planted a garden. In it were beans and squash and peppers and tomatoes and peas and carrots and corn and potatoes.

In the meadow, the old apple tree was covered with blossoms because of Ira's pruning. In the summer, Ira and Edward canned the vegetables from the garden and sold them, too, to the townspeople, along with the cheese and the eggs. And Ira bought a good wagon from a farmer, and the horse tossed his head as he pulled the wagon into town, where Edward and Ira bought feed and oats and all the other things they needed.

So several years passed. Edward was no longer sure of the exact spot where the pigsty had been. He hardly ever thought of it anymore. He had grown tall and strong, and he could carry more wood than the old man. He could read nearly everything, and he could add and multiply and divide. He had learned to cook as well as Ira did, and to sew and mend socks, as well as mend the horse's harness. With each new thing he learned, he wanted to learn more.

On a hot August afternoon, a violent thunderstorm came to the valley. It split open the sky, and tumbled rocks from the slopes of the hills, and tore the little green apples off the apple tree. It frightened the chickens and set the nanny goat to bleating and the horse to neighing. The cat, Jennie, hid under the bed, and the sky grew as black as night.

Edward's head was filled with images of slowly turning things like the sun and moon, of paths leading to faraway places, and streams becoming rivers, and he knew that, long ago, he had had just such thoughts. And as he was trying to put all the new words he had learned to these curious visions, he thought he heard the thunder mumble, "They are coming back!"

"I think they will be back soon," he said to Ira Winks. Ira nodded, as though he knew exactly what Edward was talking about.

The next morning dawned fresh and calm. Edward harnessed up the horse and wagon to go to town and buy soap and kerosene and cheesecloth and chicken feed.

When he got to the store, the storekeeper, who knew him well by now, said, "Edward, I've heard a strange story this day. Several folk have told me they saw an old couple sheltering in a hen coop on the other side of town. They are ragged and sick and have nothing. It was said that they are the Gudges, with whom you lived so many years ago."

At once, Edward remembered everything. Pigs. The gray walls of the cottage, the earth floor, the damp and the cold, the hard bread and crumbly cheese.

His heart beat painfully. "It can't be them!" he cried.

"It's nearly certain it is," said the storekeeper.

"If it *was* the Gudges, they would have come straight to the cottage and claimed everything for themselves," protested Edward. But he knew he was only trying to wish away the truth.

"I was told they are too feeble to go one step farther than they did," said the storekeeper.

At first, Edward was miserable. Then, as he loaded up the wagon, he grew angry. They would turn everything back to the way it had been! He would lose his name! He would be the little swineherd again! He flung a great sack of chicken feed into the wagon.

At that very second, he realized the truth. He was no longer little. No one could turn him back into a little swineherd! And then he remembered that though the Gudges had not been kind to him, they had not been very cruel, either. So he headed the horse to the other side of town. Soon he saw an old hen coop, its slats broken, its roof caved in, and, huddled against its sunny side, an ancient man and an ancient woman who looked like two scarecrows.

He stood wordlessly before them for a long time before they became aware of his presence and looked up at him. Then the old woman said in a whining voice, "Would you have something to eat, sir? A little thing you could spare two starving, pitiful old folk?"

Edward went to the wagon and brought back the sandwiches he had made for his own lunch and gave them to the old woman. After the Gudges had finished every crumb, they appeared to gain strength, and they stood up. The old woman stared closely at Edward's face.

"Why, I do believe you're our little swineherd!" she exclaimed. "That's exactly who you are! And that's our old horse!"

"Yes," said Edward.

"You must drive us home directly," she ordered. "We've been too weak to go a step farther than this hateful hen coop. But all that is changed now. And it's a lucky thing for *you* that it has!"

For *him,* thought Edward as the old couple got into the wagon. They looked at him expectantly as he looked back at them; then Mrs. Gudge said crossly, "Hurry up! We've waited long enough."

When they drove through the town, people came out to stare. As they went down the road toward the cottage, Edward tried to think of what he could do.

"I heard that you were traveling around the world," he said to Mrs. Gudge.

"The world is not what it is cracked up to be," she replied sharply. "And furthermore, you are only a swineherd, although it's true that you are no longer little, and I'm not obliged to tell you of our change of plans."

"I want some porridge," said the old man crankily. "And I want all this chatter to stop."

After that everyone was silent until they came to the cottage. Around it grew the flowers that Ira Winks had planted, and in front of it stood the little yellow stand with the sign that said "eggs" and "cheese," and in the garden the great green leaves of the squash gleamed in the sunlight, and there stood Ira Winks speaking softly to the nanny goat.

The old woman stood straight up in the wagon.

"Pigs!" she cried. "Where are my pigs!"

"And my pigs, too!" shouted the old man.

Edward jumped down from the wagon, and Ira walked toward him, and they both looked at Mr. and Mrs. Gudge.

"You've stolen our home," Mrs. Gudge accused them.

"You've fixed up our barn," said Mr. Gudge.

"And eaten up all the pigs," said Mrs. Gudge.

"And gone into trade on *our land*," said Mr. Gudge.

"And we've lined your old cupboard with jars and jars of pennies," said Ira Winks, "and put a plow in your barn and a floor in your cottage, and pruned the old apple tree, and gotten a rooster, and sent your ward to school to learn to read and write and do numbers so he can take his place in the world."

"He's not our ward," said Mrs. Gudge.

"He's just a foundling," said Mr. Gudge.

"And if it hadn't been for us—" the old man began.

"Why, it was the luckiest day in his life when we found him!" cried the old woman.

"Let's see the pennies," said the old man, and he hopped out of the wagon so energetically it was hard for Edward to believe that only a short time ago he'd been crumpled up against the side of a collapsed hen coop.

"What are we to do?" Edward whispered to Ira as Mr. and Mrs. Gudge ran to the cottage.

"I think it may be time to go West," said Ira Winks.

They watched the Gudges from the cottage door as the old couple ran from corner to corner, counting pennies and jars, lifting quilts, exclaiming, complaining, interrupting each other. The dust flew out from their clothes, and they appeared to be getting stronger every minute.

"You got tired of the world?" asked Ira Winks at last.

"Why, your eyes don't match," observed the old woman as she snatched up a jar of tomatoes.

"And I want my porridge," said Mr. Gudge.

"We have no reason to speak to *you,*" said Mrs. Gudge to Ira Winks, "whatever you are."

Edward thought—the cottage had changed, the apple tree had changed, the pigsty had changed, and he himself had changed most of all. But there were things, he saw, that never changed, and he stared at Mr. and Mrs. Gudge and thought of them as he had found them, pitiful heaps of bones and rags by the side of the road, and look at them now! As greedy and irritable as they'd always been!

"We're going West," he said. "And we are leaving you your fine cottage and good barn, and everything that is in them except for the old horse that we've taken care of all the years of your absence, and our cat, Jennie, whose tail you just stepped on, and Ira's goat. And we'll take the kettle and a few supplies and all the clothes we made, and the wagon we bought with the pennies we earned with our labor, and consider that this is the luckiest day of your life because we don't close the cottage door and leave you to wander forever."

"Just so," agreed Ira Winks, and, without paying any more attention to the Gudges, Edward and Ira began to load up the wagon with all the things Edward had claimed. Then Ira went to the barn and brought back three jars of pennies, which he had kept there near the horse stall as their savings.

"I thought they might come back someday," said Ira. "So I put these aside to help us along until we get to the West."

After that they harnessed up the old horse and put Jennie in a basket into the wagon and the goat next to her, and Ira filled a lantern with kerosene and hung it on the wagon. Then they looked back at the Gudges through the open door of the cottage. The old couple were piling up food on the table, everything they could find, and were babbling at each other and gobbling just as Edward remembered they used to do while he was feeding the pigs their slops.

The old horse pulled the wagon through the soft, sweet summer twilight, and Ira and Edward did not speak for a long time, for it is a hard thing to start all over again, and they were both thinking their own thoughts. Then Ira said, "You'll miss your school friends and Mrs. Henry."

"Yes," agreed Edward. "Especially Flora and Luke."

"You left the cottage better than it was when you first came to it," said Ira.

"We did that," said Edward.

"One should always leave a place better than one finds it," Ira remarked, "although that is not always possible."

"Where *is* West?" asked Edward. He had never asked Ira Winks that before.

"Far," replied Ira. "But not too far for us."

The nanny goat bleated softly in the back of the wagon, and, because it was growing dark, Ira lit the lantern.

Edward wondered.

The goose looked at the surface of the pond that was full of the light of sunset. The reeds rustled. She sighed and said, "I must be off. It has gotten quite late."

"That's an interesting story," said the duck. "But there are a few points I'd like to bring up. Who were Edward's real parents? And don't you think you can be more specific about *West*? Anything could be West, after all."

"I don't know who Edward's parents were," answered the goose. "And *West* could be anything. You're quite right."

"But what was Edward wondering about there at the end?" asked the duck somewhat impatiently.

"Everything," answered the goose.

The duck felt put out. "I notice you mention geese a lot in your story," he said accusingly.

"Well, they just happened to fly through at the time I mentioned them," said the goose, and she yawned.

"I hope you do understand that if I'm to be your manager, I will have to make a suggestion or two. Do you have a nice short story? Very, very short?"

The goose stretched out one of her great white wings, then folded it like a fan next to her body.

"Do you know about the ants and the grasshopper? I expect you've heard about how industrious the ants were, and how practical, and how the grasshopper was so frivolous and frittered away the summer. Then winter came, and the poor fellow hadn't a thing to eat while the ants were munching away on ant food and living comfortably."

"Everyone knows that story," replied the duck, who didn't.

"There's a part of it, though, that's often left out," the goose went on. "You see, one of the ants found the grasshopper absolutely charming! He made caps of morning dew and let them melt on his head. He lay in the meadow and sang songs he made up. He turned somersaults and fell over with laughter at his own jokes. He made mustaches and wigs out of grass, and he startled bees. And he made comical faces at the ants as they marched back and forth being pleased with themselves. And he imitated crickets and even field mice, and he practiced his leaping until he became the greatest leaper of all—but only because it amused him.

"The ant did her work—she had to, she was an ant—but secretly she put aside little stores of food for the grasshopper, and secretly she watched him whenever her supervisor wasn't watching *her,* and she often smiled in the dark ant tunnels, just thinking of the gaiety of the grasshopper, and his sunny foolishness.

"The autumn came, and then the cold set in, and the ants burrowed away in their snug places, but she went off to look for the grasshopper, whom she found, at last, shivering under a dried-up maple leaf.

" 'I've come to live with you and take care of you,' she said, 'because you're such a prize.'

" 'What luck!' cried the grasshopper. And the ant took care of him, and he danced and sang his songs for her and told her the jokes he made up, and they lived in quite a happy way for some time."

"Not forever?" asked the duck disapprovingly.

"There's no such thing," observed the last frog, who had stayed late to listen. Then he jumped with a small plop into the water.

"I really must go now," said the goose.

"I'll need a few more samples before I can offer you terms," said the duck.

"Tomorrow," said the goose. "Tomorrow I'll be back here to tell the frogs the story of the rooster who could not see enough of himself."

"The frogs!" protested the duck. "What about me?"

"Oh—you're welcome, too," answered the goose, and flew off into the last rays of the sunset.

The following afternoon, the duck returned to the clump of reeds on the edge of the pond. He found the goose just settling down among the frogs, who were lined up as before on their water-lily pads.

"I'm here," said the duck. "You can begin."

"She doesn't need your permission to begin," remarked one of the frogs.

The duck started to make an angry reply, but the goose said, "Never mind. The story is the thing." And she began.

The Rooster Who Could Not See Enough of Himself

If the farmer's wife had not bought a new rocking chair, the farmer would not have carried the old rocking chair to the attic. And if he had not gone to the attic, he would not have seen how cluttered and dusty and jumbled it was. And if he had not decided to clean out the attic, once and for all, he would not have loaded up the wagon with things to throw in the dump down the road. And if he had not been in such a hurry to get the work done, he would not have carried so many heaps of things at once. And if he had not been carrying such heaps of things all at once, he would not have dropped a little old mirror near the barnyard, where it lodged itself at the base of a rock that held it upright so that a young chicken scratching in the dirt nearby caught a glimpse of herself. And if she hadn't seen herself, neither would the rooster have seen himself.

But the farmer did take the old rocking chair up to the attic to store, and then everything else happened, too.

The young chicken knew nothing about mirrors and their power to reflect. She thought she was being made fun of by her twin sister. She pecked at the glass, cracked her beak, and gave a great squawk.

"Old Hen," she cried, running toward the coop, "there is something strange and bad in the barnyard!"

The Old Hen, who had been taking an afternoon nap, opened one eye. "It may not be bad just because it's strange," she observed.

But the other chickens, who might have been just as wise as the Old Hen but were not as tired, began to run all over the yard, crying, "What? What's happened? Tell us!"

"An event!" exclaimed a Muscovy duck.

"It can have nothing to do with me," mumbled a pig, his snout buried in a bucket of slops. "Because," he added, gulping, "it's not something to eat or else they would be eating it!"

Several crows, who were planning how best to destroy the farmer's crops, observed the turmoil in the yard from a nearby tree and remarked among themselves how silly all earthbound fowl were, running about and shrieking all because of a bit of glass.

Some sheep grazing in the meadow raised their heads at all the noise, but they didn't think anything at all.

"What's going on here?" asked the rooster, who regarded himself as the only sensible creature for miles around. "I say, what is all the fussing about?"

"Over there!" shouted the young chicken who had seen herself in the mirror. For once, she felt as important as the rooster.

He sauntered casually over to the mirror, aware that all eyes were watching him.

"It's nothing at all, you foolish thing," he said to the young chicken. Then he caught sight of his reflection, and he flew back in alarm.

"A foreigner," he cried.

But the Old Hen, who had been looking on thoughtfully, said, "I believe what you saw is yourself. It's something like a pool of water, only frozen."

Cautiously, the rooster peered into the mirror. He winked his right eye. The mirror rooster winked back. He flapped his wings, and so did the mirror rooster.

"I had no idea," he murmured.

"No idea about what?" asked the young chicken.

"That I was so splendid!" exclaimed the rooster. Then he looked reproachfully at all the animals in the yard. "Not one of you ever took the trouble to tell me," he said.

The Old Hen fluffed her feathers and sighed. What a silly bird the rooster was, she thought. She started back toward the coop, glad the

rooster had something to occupy his time. He'd always been an interfering sort of creature, asking everyone what they were doing and where they were going and what they were thinking about from dawn until dusk.

Several hens tried to see themselves in the mirror, but the rooster cried, "Get back! Get back! This wonderful frozen water is not for the likes of you!"

All day long, he strutted up and down in front of the mirror, exclaiming at the thickness of his feathers, the length of his feet, the curve of his toes, and, most of all, the color of his comb and wattles, such a perfect red, so much more beautiful than the red of the sunset!

When it grew too dark for him to see himself, he began to rebuke the hens for not telling him how handsome he was.

"All these years," he said, "and not a word from any of you! I suppose you were afraid you would lose me if I found out about myself—that I might leave and go where I would be appreciated. Selfish! That's what you all are!"

The next day, the hens followed him about.

"Precious thing!" cried one.

"More lovely than the yellow grains of corn!" insisted another.

"Our barnyard beauty!" exclaimed a third. They were eager to keep him in a good temper. He was very unpleasant when he was cross, driving them away from the feed the farmer's wife threw them in the morning, or flying at them angrily for no reason at all.

But despite their compliments, the rooster felt sulky and unfairly treated. Whenever he was near the hens, he pretended to be talking to himself. "A talent like mine—and these ignorant fowl unable to appreciate it. . . . Or worse! They knew all along! And kept it from me!"

He heard the crows muttering in the tree. "What dull-looking birds," he murmured. He watched the Muscovy duck taking a morning swim in the little pond. "He can't even quack," he said.

"Muscovy ducks aren't supposed to quack," said the Old Hen, who happened to be passing by. The rooster started to reply, when he saw the young chicken looking at herself in the mirror.

"How dare you!" he shouted, rushing at her. She scurried away, and the rooster took his accustomed place in front of the mirror.

"Yes . . . you're just as I remember," he said to his image. "I had thought it was all a dream. Just look at that comb! Can it have gotten redder since yesterday?"

Later, he took a walk near the sheep. "Even such lowly animals deserve a treat," he said to himself, pleased with his own generosity. But the sheep didn't look up from their grazing. "Some creatures are afraid of being dazzled," declared the rooster, for he almost always had an answer to any doubt that entered his mind.

For the first time in his life, the rooster began to look at the countryside. If only there were some high place where he could climb! Then everyone would be able to see him and admire him. But the land was as flat as a platter. Even flatter. It was so discouraging!

He brooded. Then he went back to the mirror and felt comforted.

The hens, the chickens, and the Muscovy duck had begun to avoid the rooster as much as was possible in a crowded place like a barnyard. The Old Hen tried to warn him.

"Be careful!" she said. "If you go on like this, you'll forget there's anything more to you than the way you look! Even your crowing is not what it used to be. It was decidedly feeble this morning."

The rooster was bewildered. Forget himself? Why, himself was all he ever thought of!

"You have no feeling for beauty," he said somewhat timidly. He was a little afraid of the Old Hen. "I am interested only in the exceptional radiance of my comb and wattles," he explained.

"You were born with that comb and those wattles," replied the Old Hen. "And it's nothing you can take credit for, any more than you can take credit for the sunshine or the tassels on the corn in the field, or the cool dust you scratch in."

She walked off, shaking her head.

Well, thought the rooster, he couldn't expect that everyone would prize him. He cleared away a few pebbles that had rolled up against the base of the mirror. Ah! Now he could see his slim ankles, the delicate ruffle of his leg feathers. Suddenly, he caught a glimpse of the farm cat staring at him from behind a fence. He flew at her, wings outstretched, crowing his fiercest.

How satisfying it was to him to see the cat retreat and slink around the corner of the farmhouse!

"He's eaten locoweed," remarked the cat to herself.

The rooster continued to ponder the problem of how to make himself more visible. But there wasn't a hill around as far as he could see, not a slope, not even a mound. He supposed he could get on the plow horse's back, but when the horse wasn't in the barn, he was out working the fields. There'd be no point in that.

But the solution was right there in front of him! The barn! It loomed high above him. If he could somehow get to the roof, he was sure he would be seen by all the animals in the country. He owed it to everyone, didn't he? One chance to see something really sublime!

But the barn presented a problem. How was he to reach the roof? He could fly, of course, but not very far and not very high up.

The Muscovy duck and the Old Hen were watching him from a few feet away.

"What's he up to now?" wondered the Muscovy duck. "He's getting absolutely unbearable, you know. Perhaps we could hide that thing from him."

"Not yet," said the Old Hen. "It would only make him worse."

"I can't see how that's possible," complained the duck.

"What are you up to?" called the Old Hen to the rooster.

"I'm thinking," replied the rooster with dignity.

"I doubt you can fly to the roof," said the Old Hen.

"I wish he'd maroon himself on a rafter in the barn with the bats," muttered the Muscovy duck. "Exactly where he belongs. . . ."

"I had no intention of flying to the roof," said the rooster, "although if I had, I'd certainly find a way."

He regretted his boasting at once. If anyone could help him, the Old Hen could. She was hard-hearted, but she was clever.

Later, after the Muscovy duck had gone to the pond, the rooster said to her, "If I *did* want to get to the roof, how would you suggest I go about it? I have my own ideas, naturally, but I'm interested in anything you have to offer."

The Old Hen said, "I might be able to persuade the sheep to help." She looked at him sternly. "But only if you promise on your word of honor that you will stop all this nonsense with the frozen water from the moment you get down from the roof."

"Oh, yes!" cried the rooster. "I promise, I promise anything."

"Let me think about it," said the Old Hen. "Tomorrow morning, I'll see what I can do."

The rooster was pleased with himself. Along with everything else, he had become shrewd. Look how he'd persuaded the Old Hen to help him!

The next morning, he watched the Old Hen speaking to the sheep, who grumbled and kicked up their heels but followed her back to the barnyard.

"They've agreed to help," she told the rooster. "I once did them a favor long ago."

The sheep marched right up to the side of the barn. Four of them lined up, then three leaped to the backs of the four, then two leaped to the backs of the three, then one very thin young ewe backed up several yards, took a great running jump, and landed on the backs of the two sheep.

"They won't get you all the way to the top," said the Old Hen, "but far enough so that you can make it on your own."

Without a further word, the rooster raced to the sheep ladder and, using their hindquarters as rungs, found himself within a few feet of the barn roof. Without a second's hesitation, he took off, crowing with pride at the thought of his approaching glory, and landed on the roof edge. He heard the sheep baaing as they thudded, one by one, to the ground, and he felt the old shingles crackling like little flames as he made his way to the top of the barn.

The sky had never looked more blue or more grand. Below, he saw the farmlands stretching to the horizon, green and gold fields, ponds

and woods, barns and farmhouses. A rusty weather vane creaked as it shifted in the breeze. The rooster opened his wings and crowed as loud as he was able.

The farmer and his wife, who were standing at the back door of the farmhouse, looked up.

"Great day!" exclaimed the farmer. "That rooster of ours has got himself on the barn roof!"

"How will he ever get down?" asked his wife.

"If he got up, he can get down," the farmer answered. "I haven't got the time to go up and get him."

"Quite so," remarked his wife.

The rooster, who had no intention of getting down, listened to the echoes of his crowing, and when they had died away, he waited for the response he had been dreaming of. There was no applause; there were no cries of appreciation. A short time later, two sparrows flew by. "There are two weather vanes down there, did you notice?" said one.

"I prefer the silent one, don't you?" replied the other.

The rooster crowed himself hoarse. Nothing happened at all. "The trouble with animals is that they never look up," the rooster said loudly. And then he told himself—the day was too bright, the roof was too high, the crows were making too much noise. But when the shadow of the weather vane began to lengthen across the roof, he told himself the truth.

"I'm too small to be seen," he muttered. It was a downright shame, but there was nothing to be done about it.

"Old Hen?" he called. "I'm coming down. Call back the sheep."

"I only did them *one* favor," replied the Old Hen. "You'll have to get down by yourself."

"But I can't!" cried the rooster, peeking over the edge of the roof. "It's too far!"

"It is a bit of a drop," admitted the Old Hen. "But there's nothing to be done about it. None of us can help you."

The sun set. Night came. The rooster heard the bats stirring under the roof on their rafters in the barn. It was a moonless night. Surely he would be rescued! There wasn't even a place on the roof for a rooster to roost. He made himself as snug as he could near the weather vane, somewhat comforted by its creaking as the night wind turned it back and forth.

The sun rose at last. The rooster heard the familiar sounds of the barnyard as the animals awoke and went about their business. He could see the Muscovy duck taking his morning swim in the pond.

"They'll realize what they've lost after I'm dead and gone," said the rooster. But he wasn't really sure.

All day long, he walked back and forth along the edge of the roof. The ground looked farther away each time he looked. He simply couldn't do it!

On the third day, a crow came and perched a few feet away from him.

"You're looking pale," observed the crow. "Don't you think you'd better get back to your own turf? I've heard there's a heat wave on its way."

"I'm thinking," said the rooster with dignity. "I came up here to think."

"Ha! Ha! Ha!" cawed the crow. "Thinking, are you!" And laughing raucously, the crow flew back to the tree to report on the rooster to the other crows.

The rooster caught a fly. "Not very tasty," he said mournfully. "Up here, things aren't as nice as they are on the ground."

The sun's rays grew hotter. There was no place for the rooster to shelter, and he began to fear that he would melt. The next day was even worse. He began to imagine the roof shingles were smoking. For once, the crows were quiet. The Muscovy duck did not go for his swim. The hens did not cluck. That night, there was a great rainstorm. The rooster had never been so wretched in his life. He shook and trembled and huddled next to the weather vane, which was, after all, better than nothing. And he began to think of all the unkind ways he had treated the other creatures in the barnyard. Now he understood why they wouldn't help him! He had been a rooster tyrant. He had taken the best things to eat for himself. He had ordered everyone around ever since he could remember, demanding this and demanding that. Then the frozen water had come, and he had hogged it all. And what did he ever talk about? Himself! No wonder they were glad to be rid of him!

"I see it all now," he said to the weather vane as a pale, watery-looking sun rose in the east. "I'm vain and disagreeable even though I have the most beautiful wattles and comb ever seen in the land."

With these words, he walked to the edge of the roof and cast himself off, sure that the tree where the crows roosted would be the last thing he ever saw.

But to his astonishment, he floated earthward gently and, in two seconds, felt the cool dust between his long toes.

He looked all around. The sheep were off grazing in the meadow. The hens were pecking at the grain the farmer's wife had brought them. The pig was taking a mud bath. The Muscovy duck was just emerging from the pond.

"How brave I am!" thought the rooster. "How ridiculous to think that a creature as smart as I am couldn't get down from that barn roof!" He had forgotten all his regrets of the night before. And he had forgotten his promise to the Old Hen. For, at once, not even stopping to pick up a kernel or two of corn, he rushed to the mirror, his chest swelling with anticipation. And then—

"I've been faded!" he screamed, and collapsed in a heap, sobbing wildly and covering his head with his wings. For a long time, he wept. Then he sniffled. Then he just lay there in front of the mirror.

"Congratulations on your jump," said the Muscovy duck on his way to the barn.

"I was sure you'd get down," said the Old Hen. "But I see you have already broken your promise. Why are you resting there in front of the frozen water?"

The rooster raised his head. "I am not what I was," he said sadly. "Look at my comb and wattles. The red has gone."

It was true. The rooster's comb and wattles were white.

Perhaps it had been the heat; perhaps the rain; perhaps it had been the fear he had felt just before he jumped.

The hens looked at him sympathetically. The young chicken said, to comfort him, "You *are* very tall."

He stood up, his tail feathers dragging on the ground. "I think I'll go and rest—that is, if it won't disturb any of you," he said, and he walked ever so humbly to the henhouse, where he hid himself in the dark among the nests.

The Old Hen stared at the mirror. Then she plucked it from the rock with her beak and walked to the edge of the little pond. There she flung the mirror as far as she could and waited until it had sunk from sight.

She was sure the rooster would recover some of his old spirit and find something especially distinguished about his new bleached condition. There are so many ways to find oneself beautiful, she thought.

I've heard there are white frogs in caves in the earth," remarked one of the frogs when the goose ended the story.

The duck said, "That poor rooster! What he needed was a vehicle —a good play or a revue act in which he could have starred."

"I don't agree," said another frog. "He wouldn't have been willing to learn anyone else's lines."

The duck ignored the frog. "There are one or two things," he said to the goose. "For example, what was the favor the hen had done for the sheep?"

"She scared off a fox when the ewes were lambing," replied the goose.

"But did the red ever come back to the rooster's comb and wattles?" asked the duck.

"Oh, yes," said the goose. "In time, the color returned. But the rooster had really changed, so it didn't matter."

"The story might go," said the duck. "But I think it needs a few more details. How about throwing in some anecdotes from your own life? That's what an audience really likes to hear."

"I can't see the point of that," said the goose.

"You aren't in show business," said the duck.

"I must be going," said the goose.

"Will you come back?" asked the duck.

"For a few more days," said the goose.

The frogs jumped off the lily pads one by one.

"I liked the Muscovy duck," remarked the duck. "A very dignified sort of animal."

The goose began to spread her wings.

"What's the story for tomorrow?" the duck asked.

"I think I'll tell you a story about circles and straight lines," replied the goose.

"Promising," said the duck, who hadn't the least idea what the goose was talking about.

The duck spent the night sneezing in an abandoned hen coop not far from the pond.

"Phoo!" he exclaimed in the morning, his eyes watering and his beak itching from the dust and old chicken feathers that rose from the ground each time he sneezed. "What terrible housekeepers chickens are," he observed to himself. "But beggars can't be choosers. . . ." And he poked around in the earth, finding a few stale grains of corn for his breakfast. He waddled outside.

A soft rain was falling, but it was a cold rain, and the duck shivered at the thought of the winter that was coming. He was sure that animals with steady work never had his worries. If only he could convince the goose of the charm of a life spent in the entertainment world, the excitement of unknown audiences, the thrill of applause! But then, because the duck was really an honest fowl—at least, sometimes—he muttered to himself, ". . . And the elegant accommodations and sumptuous meals provided by a grateful public," and he smiled sadly at the desolate little coop.

Later, the rain stopped and the air grew warmer. When the duck parted the reeds, the frogs had already taken their seats, and the goose was sitting quietly in their midst.

"Sorry if I'm late," said the duck. "I had a few business details to take care of." Actually, he had napped for some time beneath a willow tree.

"You're not late," said the goose in her kindly way. "I was only just about to begin."

"What's all this about circles and straight lines?" asked the duck in a somewhat lofty voice.

A frog giggled.

"You'll see," replied the goose. "Now, listen."

Circles and Straight Lines

Once upon a time there was a pony whose job it was to turn a millstone that ground up grain into coarse flour. Every morning, he was hitched up to a stout pole that was connected to a rough stone disk which, as the pony moved, crushed the grain against a smooth stone disk. All day long, he walked in a circle, knowing that, after he had walked a certain time, he would be unhitched from the stout pole, given a bucket of oats as satisfying as the one he got in the morning, and led back to his stall in the barn.

A cricket who amused himself by making startling suggestions to any animal who would listen to him hopped to the pony's ear.

"Why spend your life going round in circles?" he whispered. "Why not try going straight ahead?"

"I never thought of that," replied the pony, who had, in fact, spent a number of years not thinking about anything.

"Tomorrow, before your master comes to take you from the barn, simply walk out. Yes, yes! Walk out into the light and keep going into the world! How does that strike you?"

"But I won't know where to go," said the pony. "And I have never been out in the world."

"I will accompany you," said the cricket. "It is warm and pleasant here, next to your ear. Besides, autumn is coming and I have nothing better to do."

The next morning, just as the barn owl closed his eyes, just as the purple grackle flew to a fence post near the cowshed, the pony slipped out of the barn. He started off at once toward the millstone.

"No, no!" exclaimed the cricket. "Go in the opposite direction! That is your whole trouble. You do the same thing every day."

"But I thought everyone did the same thing every day," said the pony as he trotted down the road away from the farm and the barn and the grindstone.

"Do you really think that *every* pony has a cricket nestling next to his ear?" asked the cricket. "Think! Something unusual began to happen to you the instant we met!"

The pony said, "It is very odd to walk this way. It makes me feel as though I were about to fall off the edge of something or other."

"Something or other is the beginning of the world," said the cricket. "And you can't possibly fall off it. Keep your head up! I notice you have a tendency to veer to the right or to the left. Of course, that will pass in time, after you get used to going in a straight line, straight ahead, forward, onward, and so forth."

"I am going forth," said the pony.

"Correct," affirmed the cricket.

The sun grew warmer. A mockingbird sang among the copper-colored leaves of a tree. The pony continued to feel peculiar. An impulse to turn, now and then, made him stumble.

"Are you enjoying this?" asked the cricket.

The pony reflected. "I don't know," he said at last. Then he added, "It is certainly different from what I'm used to."

"You must not be an old stick-in-the-mud," advised the cricket, pleased to instruct such an ignorant creature.

"I haven't had my breakfast," said the pony rather wistfully.

"There you go again! Thinking of mundane things like food!" said the cricket, who was hardly ever hungry, especially at this time of the year.

At that moment a dog, his coat damp from a swim in the brook and a run in the meadow, appeared a few yards in front of the pony. The dog panted, gulped, wagged his tail, shook his fur, scratched, and then began to circle around and around as he prepared to take a little morning sleep.

"Look at that!" exclaimed the pony. "There's an animal that turns in a circle!"

"Only when it is tired," replied the cricket. "In any case, that particular creature, who happens to be a dog, is not a good example of anything. Dogs are so foolish they are given to chasing their own tails in the mistaken notion that their tails are not part of themselves."

The dog opened one eye. "Where are you off to?" he asked the pony.

"We are going straight ahead," answered the pony.

The dog looked about but saw no one except the pony. "I think I'll join you," he said. He was not really tired yet, as it was only the beginning of the day.

The cricket said, "You shouldn't have told him anything. Dogs are simpleminded, and they follow anything and then forget why they are following—if they knew in the first place, that is."

"I simply answered the dog's question," said the pony.

"What did you say?" asked the dog, who had imagined he was the only animal who talked to himself.

"I was speaking to a cricket in my ear," said the pony.

"Ah . . ." said the dog. "Of course, a cricket. . . ." He was silent a moment, then asked, "Is that like a flea in one's bonnet?"

"Don't laugh," ordered the cricket. "You will only encourage him. Dogs consider themselves witty and should not be encouraged in such illusions."

"I'm not laughing," protested the pony to the cricket. "I don't even know what a bonnet is."

"Where did you say we were going?" asked the dog.

"Out into the world," replied the pony.

"Great Sirius!" exclaimed the dog. "And all these years I thought I was already in the world!"

"What a coarse creature," observed the cricket.

At that moment, a black snake slid out of the grass by the side of the road and prepared herself to enjoy a little sun.

"Look at that!" cried the pony. "Another creature making a circle!"

"She is merely admiring the sheen of her scales in the sunlight," explained the cricket.

"What are you all up to?" asked the snake of the pony as she tucked her tail neatly beneath her.

"We're going straight ahead and out into the world," said the pony.

"I think I'll come along," said the snake. "I don't feel much like coiling at the moment."

"Is there breakfast up ahead?" the pony asked the cricket.

"I ate last week," said the snake with satisfaction, "and will need nothing for some time."

"I had two pieces of dry corn bread and a bowl of milk," remarked the dog, "and it was all simply delicious."

The cricket told the pony, "You must stop thinking about your stomach. There are far more important things to think about."

"My stomach is going out into the world with the rest of me," said the pony.

The dog snickered. The snake remarked, "I have the longest stom-ach of anyone I've ever met."

At that moment, a waltzing mouse, singing at the top of her lungs, flinging out her arms, bowing and circling wildly, dashed in front of the pony a few yards ahead.

"But look!" shouted the pony. "Still another creature that moves in circles!"

"She is only dizzy from being pursued all night by an owl," said the cricket crankily.

"Tra-la-la . . ." trilled the mouse; then, observing the group of animals trotting, walking, and slithering toward her, she stood still.

"Where are you all going?" she asked, keeping a sharp eye on the snake.

"Straight ahead in a straight line into the world," replied the pony.

"What a good idea!" said the mouse, still invigorated by her morning dance. "I would like to go with you—but—" and she looked uncertainly at the snake.

"Do join us," said the snake. "I've already eaten and will not be hungry for another week, by which time we will have arrived at our destination."

"What a windy snake," said the cricket. "You'd think she had nothing to do but talk, talk, talk all day long!"

"I like to listen to her," said the pony. "I like the way she knows exactly when she'll be hungry again."

"Who is that pony speaking to?" the waltzing mouse asked the dog.

"He says he has a cricket in his ear," replied the dog, and they both burst into laughter.

Two meadowlarks flying to a currant bush to pick a few currants heard the laughter and dipped down.

"Look at that crew!" said one. "What on earth are they doing and where do you suppose they are going?"

"They may know something we don't know," said the other meadowlark. "Let us fly along with them."

The cricket looked up at the birds, then down at the road.

"We've become a mob," he said crossly. "This is not at all what I had in mind."

Suddenly, the snake cried, "Halt for ant crossing!"

All the animals waited while a column of ants made its way from one side of the road to the other. Then, just as the pony lifted his foot to start walking again, the ant column turned and started back across the road to where it had begun its march.

"Now, look at that!" cried the pony. "Those creatures don't go in a straight line, not for long, anyhow. See how they're circling back?"

"They've forgotten something," said the cricket. "Ants are famous for forgetting something."

Just as the column reached the middle of the road, the leader of the ants looked up at the waltzing mouse.

"What is the meaning of this parade?" it asked. "Only ants are permitted to hold parades."

"Who says?" demanded the dog.

"We say," replied the ant.

"We say. . . ." murmured the column of ants.

"We are going out into the world in a straight line," explained the pony.

"We can do that," said the ant leader. "We think we'll come along."

"We'll come along," echoed the ant column.

"No!" shouted the cricket, but his shout was so tiny that only the pony heard him. "Please!" pleaded the cricket. "Remind the ant that it was crossing the road! Enough is enough!"

"Weren't you on your way across the road?" asked the pony of the ant leader.

"Oh, that!" said the ant. "It was nothing—just a passing thought we all had."

". . . all had," whispered the ant column.

The pony with the cricket next to his ear, the dog, the snake, the waltzing mouse, the two meadowlarks overhead, and the column of ants continued straight down the road.

"Isn't it interesting to think," began the dog to the waltzing mouse, "that under ordinary circumstances, none of us would be together?"

"Wonderful!" cried the waltzing mouse. "The only danger is that one of us may become hungry."

"I'm hungry," said the pony.

The cricket had grown morose and did not bother to make a comment.

"Are you still there?" asked the pony.

"Watch your big hoofs!" cried the leader of the ants.

"Sorry," apologized the pony.

"Yes, I'm still here," said the cricket, "but this is not turning out the way I had planned."

"I hope we get to the world soon," said the pony, "because then someone might be able to spare me an oat or two."

At that moment, a cat who had been investigating a hollow tree by the side of the road turned to watch the animals pass by. "I bet they are going to a picnic," he said to himself. "Maybe they'll let me go along." And he leaped in front of the column of ants, the pony, the snake, the waltzing mouse, the dog, and the two meadowlarks overhead, and did a dazzling somersault and a brilliant cartwheel, then caught his tail in his paws and bowed to the ground.

"I give up," said the cricket.

"What a lot of creatures there are who are not in the world but who move in circles," observed the pony.

"What a jolly group!" cried the cat. "Are you going to a picnic? Can I come?"

"As long as you remember that *we're* not the picnic," said the mouse.

"Never!" shouted the cat, who had a taste for dramatic emphasis. "Never would I do in a comrade on the road!"

"We have become a spectacle," muttered the cricket.

"Is that a good thing?" asked the pony.

"Who is the pony talking to?" asked the cat of the snake.

"I've heard a rumor that he claims he has a cricket in his ear," answered the snake.

"How extraordinary!" exclaimed the cat, simply for the pleasure of saying a large word.

At that moment, something glittered so brightly in the sun that all the animals, except for the column of ants and their leader, blinked and stood still. There before them, stretching from the little prickly branches of a huge shrub to the leafy branches of an apple tree, was an immense spider's web covered with glistening drops of early-morning dew.

"But what is *that*?" asked the pony. "And look! A creature is running around it with more legs than any of us have!"

"That is a spider," answered the cricket. "And he is mending his web." He couldn't resist answering a question even when he felt glum.

"The spider moves in circles, up and down, and sometimes straight ahead," said the pony thoughtfully.

"What if it does!" exclaimed the cricket.

At that moment, the last drop of dew melted in the sunlight, and, through the now-transparent web, the pony saw his own barn, the millstone, and the house where the farmer lived with his family.

"But we're back where we started," said the pony.

The leader of the ants, who, with the column, was a few yards down the road, halted. "I've forgotten what we're doing here," it said. "Forgotten . . ." repeated the column. "Ah, well," said the leader of the ants, "we must go on, at all costs," and it led the column into a mud-hole.

The dog said, "This has been a fine morning's outing, but now I must see to the sheep I guard." He ran off.

"I haven't finished my investigation of that hollow tree," remarked the cat. He dashed off.

"I must wash my scales in the brook," said the snake. "Thank you all for this pleasant interlude, and you, pony, may you always have a cricket in your ear." The snake chuckled throughout her whole length, and slid away.

"I have some new music to practice," said the waltzing mouse, "though I'm sure it did me good to take a little time for roaming." She circled away.

The two meadowlarks dipped down toward the pony one last time, then they soared up into the sky.

"I wonder what they all had in mind?" said one.

"It's a mystery," said the other. They flew off to the currant bush.

"It seems we've just gone in a circle," the pony said to the cricket, "although it *was* a larger circle than I am used to."

There was no answer. The cricket, who had known all along that the road led right back to the farm, had gone to the hen yard to work mischief among the hens.

The pony trotted off to the millstone, where the farmer was waiting, standing next to a bucket of oats. The pony ate his breakfast hungrily, then the farmer hitched him up to the stout pole.

The pony began his accustomed round, and the millstones ground the wheat. For a long time, the pony thought about nothing. Then, as the sun climbed the sky to noon, he began to recall all the things that had happened to him when he left the barn just as the owl had closed his eyes and the purple grackle had flown to the fence post. "Well . . ." he said to himself with a sigh, "it's something to look forward to . . . seeing the world. . . ."

Frankly," began the duck, "I guessed the animals were *already* in the world."

"But that's the point," said one of the frogs.

"What point?" asked the duck, despite his intention never to speak directly to a frog.

All the frogs burst into laughter.

The duck was indignant at having to put up with their silly comments and their jeering. If the goose hadn't been there, he would have given them a fright they wouldn't have forgotten in a hurry.

"Of course I see the point!" he shouted. "Crickets love to work mischief!" He looked plaintively at the goose. She nodded and said, "That's a good point, too."

"I think you might throw in a few more animals," suggested the duck, somewhat calmed down. "A cow, say, and a weasel. Perhaps even a duck?"

"Why not a tyrannosaur?" said one of the frogs.

The duck was silent. He didn't know what a tyrannosaur was, but he had no intention of letting any frog know that.

"Speaking of saurians," said the goose, "tomorrow's story is about an alligator."

"Ugh!" exclaimed the duck. "I don't think we ought to include that in your repertoire. Who would love an alligator?"

"Another alligator," said a frog in a deep bass voice.

"It's time for me to leave," said the goose.

"Yes, and I must return to the café in a charming little inn I discovered—" began the duck, but the goose had already flown away, and the frogs had already jumped into the pond.

The duck waddled back to the chicken coop, hoping there were a few more grains of corn hidden among the dusty old feathers. He was certainly putting up with great hardship to convince the goose she could have a career in the theater. He stepped into the coop and, at once, began to sneeze.

The next afternoon, his spirits restored by a long sleep and a brisk swim in the pond, the duck strode through the reeds.

"Well—let's see how the alligator plays!" he said heartily.

"The alligator I am going to tell you about doesn't do any playing," said the goose. "He tells the truth."

"The truth?" asked the duck.

"The truth," repeated one of the frogs. "That's when you say what you mean and mean what you say."

The duck scowled, but he settled down to listen.

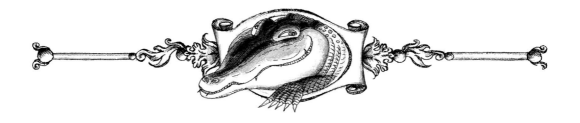

The Alligator Who
Told the Truth

Down by Mercy Landing, where the river widened and the current grew swift, there was an old wharf, a village, and a marsh. No boat had tied up to the rotting timbers of the wharf for many years. The villagers were so poor that only the mayor had a pair of matching socks. In the marsh, which had once teemed with creatures of all sorts, only a few animals lived among the cypress stumps and in the shallow streams that wound about the spongy hummocks of mud and moss.

Long ago, the villagers had taken their pirogues down those streams to hunt the muskrats and the alligators. Now, as far as anyone knew, there were only a few muskrats and one old alligator. And the last pirogue lay on its side in the village square covered with Virginia creeper. There was no one left who remembered how to make such boats, each one hewn out of a single tree trunk.

But animals from all over the country often visited the Mercy Landing marsh. The old alligator was famous, not only for his enormous mouth, but for what came out of it. He always told the truth.

"Are you a bear?" an animal would ask.

"No," the alligator would reply without opening his eyes.

"Are you bad?" another animal would ask.

"I am not bad and I am not good," the alligator would say. "I am here."

When the alligator slept in the sun, his horrible jaw on one bank of the stream, his terrible tail on the other, and his body half sunk in water, the young muskrats would run across his scaly back from bank to bank until a faint twitch of the alligator's right front foot would warn them he was waking up. They would instantly skitter away. For as interesting as the animals found the alligator, they tried to stay out of reach of those alligator jaws.

"How many teeth do you have?" asked a woodpecker.

"I am unable to count," answered the alligator in his strange, high, toneless voice.

Whenever an animal was missing in the marsh, the alligator was consulted at once.

"Do you know where the yellow-bellied fox squirrel has got to?" asked the eastern wood rat, who was a little less afraid of the alligator than the other animals were.

"I had him for lunch," the alligator said.

"And the youngest short-tailed shrew from the sassafras tree over there?"

"I never saw her."

"And would you eat me if I came two steps nearer to you?"

"Yes," said the alligator.

"And you're absolutely sure you don't know where that shrew is?"

The alligator switched his tail back and forth, and the dark swamp

water foamed up. "That is an idle question," he said. "You know I am unable to invent an answer. I am beginning to feel angry."

Later, the little shrew did turn up. She had been playing with some young muskrats and had forgotten the time.

That was how it was, and that was how it had been for years. The alligator was very, very old, and generations of shorter-lived animals had had the story of his truth-telling passed on to them. He was, really, the most important animal in the marsh because he could be trusted to say what was so, and not because he was even more dangerous than the snakes who swirled and coiled and curled through the streams and around the trunks of trees.

Sometimes the animals asked him questions of a general nature. Such questions as: Why is the marsh getting smaller and smaller? Why do some creatures fly and others crawl? Why does the great river lift up its waters and flood the land? Why does it rain? And why does the moon shine and the wind blow?

But to all such questions the alligator merely replied, "I don't know. I don't even know why I am an alligator."

"He's no philosopher," observed an eastern flying squirrel.

"And not a scientist either," said a common mole.

"He's just a stomach with teeth," said a young cotton rat.

"But he does tell the truth," said a harvest mouse, "and that is something."

"If the people in the village knew about the alligator, they'd be pouring into our marsh to ask him questions," said the common mole.

The eastern flying squirrel, who felt superior because he was a creature of both the air and the land, said, "You're quite mistaken. You know nothing of the world. The people in the village would not be interested in an animal that tells the truth. You don't know human beings the way I do. Besides, there aren't enough villagers left to pour into the marsh."

All that may or may not have been true. The fact was, the squirrel enjoyed talking more about things he didn't know than what he did know.

But shortly after this conversation, the eastern flying squirrel lost some of his reputation as an authority on human beings. For when two of them, Mr. Clogg and Mr. Fork, started creeping about the marsh, the animals were sure—at least in the beginning—that the human beings had come to visit the alligator because they had heard about his great gift.

From hollow tree trunks, from the water, from clumps of reeds, and from holes in the earth, they watched Clogg and Fork pick and poke about the marsh. Even the alligator hid himself so that no part of him showed except the tip of his nose.

But Clogg and Fork could not have spoken with the alligator even if they had wished to do so. They were researchers. They didn't talk to animals. They investigated them. They observed them, and they took notes. Sometimes they put a very small animal in a maze to see if it could get out. Sometimes they placed food in the maze to see if the small animal could find a way in to get the food. When one grew discouraged, the other would proclaim: *Hedgehogs see only yellow!* And they would be comforted. Think, Clogg would say, pointing a finger up at the ceiling of their laboratory, of all the trouble someone went to, to discover such an astounding fact! And Fork would nod solemnly. Someday, the two researchers hoped to make a discovery, although they had had no luck so far.

What a triumph it would be, they had agreed, to find out what colors an alligator could see!

"An alligator is dangerous, mysterious, and unlovable," said Clogg.

"We will surely win a medal," Fork said excitedly, "if we discover *anything* about such a creature!"

And word of the very old alligator, the last one in the country as far as anyone knew, had traveled up the river, from village to village, until it reached the big town where Clogg and Fork conducted their studies.

The villagers were overjoyed when the researchers arrived at Mercy Landing. Clogg and Fork bought everything in the general store and rented rooms for themselves and their equipment in the old board-inghouse near the wharf, which had not had a boarder for twenty years. It didn't take much to make the villagers feel rich. They all hoped Clogg and Fork would stay for months and months, and they encouraged the two researchers to keep hunting for the alligator, even giving them four false leads. Because of this, it took them several weeks to find him.

One very hot afternoon, the alligator crawled up out of the water to catch the heat of the sun.

"Look out!" warned the common mole from a nearby burrow. "Those two humans are thrashing about close by!"

"I am tired of hiding from them," replied the alligator. "They would do better to hide from me." And he fell instantly asleep, and that was how Clogg and Fork found him.

"Aha!" exclaimed Fork. "Our subject has appeared."

"He must grow accustomed to us," observed Clogg, and he threw a stone into the water. The alligator opened one eye and yawned.

"We must grow accustomed to him," said Fork.

"He is much larger than a hedgehog," said Clogg.

"And not a vegetarian," said Fork.

"So we must think of a sensible approach," suggested Clogg.

"One that will encourage his natural friendliness," said Fork, who always tried to think of the sunny side of life.

"He is not naturally friendly," said Clogg, who was more scientific, "but we can reach him through his stomach."

"I wouldn't care to do that," said Fork, and he laughed somewhat nervously.

For ten days, Clogg and Fork brought sacks of food and dumped them out on the bank where they had found the alligator. Then they watched him consume it—every bit of it.

"He has grown accustomed to us," remarked Clogg.

"He has grown accustomed to the food," said Fork, "and ignores us altogether, which is the best thing."

"They are up to something," said the eastern wood rat to the alligator. "I wouldn't swallow everything they bring you."

"You couldn't," replied the alligator. "You do not have my immense capacity for swallowing."

"What I mean," began the eastern wood rat somewhat impatiently, "is to be on your guard. I haven't seen a trap, but I suspect one."

"I am glad to be brought my dinners," said the alligator, although, as usual, his voice did not show any special gladness. "I have been rather tired lately, and it is a relief not to have to count on some animal's ignorance of my presence to get a bite to eat. I fear all of you marsh creatures have learned my ways. It happens with each generation. I get very, very tired and very, very hungry every few years until a new crop of you comes along."

The eastern wood rat felt a little discouraged. He had kindly feelings toward the old alligator—well, at least, respectful ones—and all that talk about ignorant animals and bites made him feel he was wasting his sympathy. He heard the two researchers approaching and said, "Don't say I didn't warn you!"

"Why would I say that?" asked the alligator, already emerging from the water in anticipation of what Clogg and Fork had brought him that day.

But in place of the gunnysack from which hams or chickens or great slabs of bacon had been dumped out on the bank the last ten days, the alligator was puzzled to see two large obstructions. These were cards devised by Clogg, and one was painted yellow and one was painted red.

"Oh, dear!" cried Fork. "Look! He's already rustling and scraping and scratching and whipping toward me, and I haven't got the yellow card firmly secured at all, and the red card is shaky! What shall I do?"

"Calm yourself," advised Clogg, who had remained a safe distance from the bank while Fork was setting up the cards. "He is not interested in *you*, in any case. It hardly matters if the cards are unsteady. We simply want to see which color attracts him most."

Just as Clogg finished speaking, the alligator reached the yellow card and, with a flick of his tail, knocked it down. Fork leaped backward.

"Look at that!" whispered the common mole to his sister where they were hiding behind the sassafras tree. "That huge creature can jump like a frog!"

"How irritating it is to have one's hopes disappointed," remarked the alligator to a water snake that was lying just below the bank. "I thought they'd hidden my dinner just to amuse themselves watching me hunt for it. But there was nothing there."

"Try that other object," suggested the snake. "I'm almost sure I saw them drop something behind it."

The alligator crawled to the red card, peered behind it, and found a delicious chunk of pork. He gobbled it down at once.

"Ah!" exclaimed Clogg. "He has found the food. Tomorrow, we will put it behind the red card again. If he detected a color, he will recall it. And so on and so forth, et cetera."

"How long do you think et cetera will take?" asked Fork.

"We will have preliminary data in a few weeks," replied Clogg, writing down ten pages of notes as the old alligator slid down the bank to take a snooze.

"You certainly got a lot of data from that," Fork said admiringly. "If I had written down anything, I would merely have noted that the alligator knocked down the yellow card and, finding no grub behind it, went to the red card, and—"

"That is why I am the head of our team," interrupted Clogg.

Day after day, week after week, the two researchers set up their cards; one was always red, and the other was any color that occurred to Clogg. In hidden spots around the bank, all the animals had come to watch the strange actions of the two humans.

"I've noticed something," said the short-tailed shrew. "That first week, those two gave the alligator food no matter what he did. But now, if he doesn't discover it at once, they remove the food altogether."

The eastern flying squirrel, whose specialty was explaining what he didn't understand, said, "I know exactly what they're doing. It's a new game called 'Alligator Chooses.'"

The wood rat said, "Pshaw! It's nothing of the kind! We don't know what it is. And neither does the old alligator. Have you noticed how slow he's becoming? Look at him today! You'd hardly know he was alive!"

It was true. The alligator barely seemed to move. Every few minutes, a foot would scrape through the mud and struggle for a hold, then the immense body and tail would advance an inch or so. Once in front of the two cards, the alligator would move his head from side to side and open his great jaws. Snap! Snap! And at that sound, the researchers retreated quickly from the bank, and all the animals shivered and blinked.

"I don't believe the animal sees any color at all," said Fork. "We've tried a thousand times, and he doesn't learn a thing."

"It's a challenge," said Clogg. "We must meet it by devising newer and better ways to discover his color sense. We must be bolder! We must push on! Think of the honors we will win! And I *am* encouraged! Do you realize that out of three hundred tries, he has chosen the red card one hundred and fifty-one times?"

"For goodness' sake! He had to go to one card or the other! What you say doesn't make any more sense than the alligator's actions."

"Red! That's the answer!" cried Clogg, carried away by his own enthusiasm. "And I have an idea how we can make absolutely sure. Forward, Fork!"

"I'd rather go backward," grumbled Fork, gathering up all their paraphernalia while Clogg wrote down his usual ten pages of notes.

The alligator, who, once again, had found nothing to eat, sank back in the water and then climbed to the opposite bank. He was terribly hungry. He was bewildered. He lumbered into a cypress trunk and banged his nose. He'd never done such a thing in his life. He doubted he'd be able to catch a dragonfly.

"He's getting quite thin," the short-tailed shrew mother told all her young. "We must be especially careful, all of us."

The animals of the marsh kept their distance, although they continued to question the alligator in their customary way. But he had grown silent and rarely answered them. He brooded. He could not fall asleep. He fell into the water sideways. When he heard the two humans crashing and thundering toward him through the marsh, he was filled with dread. Yet he couldn't ignore them. There was always the chance they would give him his dinner as they had done in the beginning. He had begun to suspect that he could no longer catch his own dinner. Only by closing his eyes and pretending to be a log could he feel like his old self.

Then, for a week, the two humans did not come to the marsh, and the animals returned to their customary affairs, and the alligator, although empty, began to feel better.

Clogg and Fork were scouring Mercy Landing to find the green cloth and the red cloth they needed for Clogg's new scheme. One old lady sold them her only tablecloth, which was green and still bore traces of gravy from the last really good Thanksgiving dinner anyone had eaten in the village, which had been at least twenty years before. And the mayor sold them two moth-eaten Santa Claus outfits from the distant past when the villagers had been rich enough to believe in Santa Claus. Then Clogg found several people who were happy to be paid for converting the tablecloth and the suits into long robes and peaked hats and masks.

"Now we will be able to prove my theory that the alligator can see red," said Clogg exultantly, clutching the two robes.

"Who is to wear the red?" asked Fork.

"Why, you!" exclaimed Clogg. "You are younger than I am and much sprier. Also, while he pursues you, I will be able to observe him and make notes. Observation, as we both know, my dear Fork, is the heart of scientific advancement, and it is not your strong suit."

All the animals in the marsh fled into their tunnels and burrows and hollow tree trunks when they saw the two apparitions in their peaked hats and long robes marching through the marsh, Clogg in green and Fork in red.

The eastern flying squirrel said, "This is the end! They intend to burn down our marsh or flood it and sink it!"

"Nonsense!" said the eastern wood rat. "They have simply invented a new way to torment the old alligator."

"Now," said Clogg as they neared the alligator's pool, "you must go as close to the top of the bank as you can so that he will not miss seeing you in your brilliant red robe. I will stand only a step or two behind you. And then we shall see."

"But shouldn't we stand side by side so we can be sure of which color he chooses?" asked Fork, peering down into the water, which was absolutely still. He couldn't even see the alligator's snout. "Clogg?" he said. At that second, the alligator, who had deserted his usual place near the cypress trunk, came up behind the two researchers and snapped up Clogg, peaked hat, mask, robe, and all.

"Good heavens!" shouted Fork. "It was *green* he could see all along!" But those were his last words, for the alligator lunged forward and snapped him up with the same speed and ease with which he had dispatched Clogg.

After several days, when the two researchers didn't return to their rooms in the Mercy Landing boardinghouse, the people of the village decided the two men had gone back to the big town up the river. The boardinghouse owner said the village must have a celebration in honor of Clogg and Fork and all the fine things they had left behind them, which the mayor himself would distribute among the villagers. So the

fiddler, the accordion player, and the old lady who played the triangle were gathered together to play for the party, which lasted for three days.

The alligator did not say one word for a week, but remained near his cypress trunk with his eyes shut tight.

Then, one morning, a young muskrat called out, "Are you a bear?"

"I don't know," replied the alligator sadly.

"The alligator doesn't know," the animals repeated among themselves.

"He is still telling the truth," said the eastern wood rat.

"How do *you* know?" asked the eastern flying squirrel. "He may think he is a bear and is just not saying so."

"He's confused," said the common mole. "Those two humans have tied his brain in a knot with all their carrying-on."

The young muskrat tried another question. "Are you bad or are you good?" he asked.

"I don't even know if I am here," said the alligator in a whisper.

"He has lost his gift," remarked the mother shrew. And all the animals agreed and were distressed, for even though the alligator had a fierce appetite, they had always found comfort in the way he spoke the truth, even if that truth did issue from his iron jaws. So they all decided that, from that day on, they would try to be more truthful themselves, and not say whatever it was the fashion to say, and in that way make up for the alligator's loss and their own.

I don't see how you could like someone who might make a meal out of you," said the duck.

"They admired him," said one of the frogs. "All the creatures in the marsh depended on him because he said what he meant and meant what he said."

"I'd rather he told me a little lie or two but didn't want to have me for dinner," said the duck resentfully. He couldn't get used to having frogs explain things to him.

"We must all have our dinners," remarked the frog, "even if it is inconvenient for someone else."

The goose said, "It's time for me to go."

"I'm so eager to come to an arrangement with you," said the duck. "Have you been thinking about that possibility at all? Letting me be your manager, that is? I'm convinced we'd be a success! I didn't mean any criticism of your story about the alligator—all that talk of mine about dinners . . . Ha-ha! It was really quite funny about Clogg and Fork—in a way. And I do believe in a varied repertoire. . . ."

"I don't mind if you criticize a story," said the goose. "Once I tell it, it belongs to you anyhow."

"But—what about the future? You and me? You and I? Us?"

"The future," repeated the goose softly. "Well, for the immediate future, I have one more story for you. And I'll come back tomorrow to tell it."

"What's it to be?" asked the smallest frog eagerly.

"It's to be about a raccoon who learns to play her troubles on a flute," replied the goose.

"I'd need a tuba and a bass drum," muttered the duck, "if I had to play my troubles."

The goose flew away into the deepening twilight, and the frogs jumped into the water, one by one. The duck remained among the reeds for a short while, then, thinking about dinners and alligators, began to feel hungry himself and went off to find something to eat.

That night he was awakened from a sound sleep by a great thrashing and thumping in the chicken coop.

"These accommodations are taken," he shouted into the dark.

"You wouldn't throw an aged rabbit out into the snow, would you?" cried a voice piteously.

"Snow!" exclaimed the duck with horror. "But it's not winter yet!"

"Ah . . . but it soon will be," said the voice. "I've just come from the north country, the snow at my back, the winds howling about my ears, the earth beneath my hind feet as hard as stone. Oh, what a winter we're going to have!"

"I smell something burning," said the duck in alarm.

"It's only my cigar," explained the voice. "You wouldn't begrudge an after-supper smoke to a tired old bunny, would you? Especially one that hadn't had his supper?"

"I certainly would," answered the duck. "Besides, it's nearly dawn."

"All right, then," said the rabbit, "call it a before-breakfast cigar. Not that I plan on breakfast, either." And at that the rabbit sobbed loudly.

"Don't try that out on me," said the duck, completely awake now. "I'm in the theater, and I know an act when I hear one."

"Good!" remarked the rabbit at once. "I'll save my tears for a better occasion," and he puffed away and twitched his ears. In the growing light, the two animals stared at each other. What a huge rabbit, thought the duck uneasily.

"I'll just take forty winks and be on my way," promised the rabbit. "Unless you go on *your* way," he added, and grinned. There was so much smoke inside the coop that the duck's eyes watered and he began to cough.

"Why not step outside for a breath of air," suggested the rabbit, waving a paw at the entrance of the coop. The duck started to reply, then thought better of it and staggered through the smoke until he was standing alone beneath a watery gray sky.

"What next?" he said to himself. As if it wasn't enough to put up with the condescension of frogs! Now giant rabbits were evicting him from the only shelter he had been able to find. Well—one giant rabbit.

A tremendous snore issued forth from the coop, and the duck hastened away toward the pond. With a sinking heart, he saw there was a skim of ice on the water. He fretted and stewed as he scratched about on the pond's muddy shore for a bite to eat, and he thought about all the troubles he had had in the past, and all the troubles he expected to have in the future. Even when the sun rose and melted the ice and warmed up the air, the duck kept on worrying, so it was a great relief to him to return to the clump of reeds and find the goose and the frogs awaiting him.

"The night was cool," remarked the goose.

"Not for us!" cried the smallest frog.

"I was evicted by a bear," said the duck.

"There are no bears in this district," stated the largest frog.

"Well—it was a rabbit as big as a bear," said the duck, "so it might as well have been a bear."

"Might as well have been," mocked the smallest frog. "You certainly do exaggerate. No wonder you're in show business!"

"You just wait until the blizzard comes here!" cried the duck. "You'll see who's exaggerating then! And the bears from the far north will stomp all over your lily pads and the wind will howl and the snow will bury these reeds!"

The frogs all croaked and sneered and jeered and leaped up and down, and the duck quacked and shouted until the goose rose to her full height and flapped her great wings.

"Do calm yourselves," she said. "I'm eager to tell you my last story, but I can't while you're making such a racket."

"Not my fault," muttered the duck.

"Ha!" exclaimed the smallest frog.

"My story," began the goose, "is about the time when the forests began to dwindle because human creatures chopped down the trees to build their shelters and wagons and barns and tables and chairs—"

"And chicken coops," interrupted the duck.

"Hush!" cried all the frogs at the same time. And the goose went on with her story.

The Raccoon's Song

In a northern forest of great oak trees where winter was the longest season, a family of raccoons lived in a hollow beneath a fallen tree. There were three small raccoons and a mother and a father. The father was frequently away tending to his own concerns. But in the winter, he would return to huddle and sleep with his family beneath the snow.

At the edge of the forest, human habitation was growing, and the animals who lived there had almost become used to the sound of the ax and the saw and the voices of men and women and children. But month by month, the trees were cut down and the ground was leveled and plowed for planting, and as people's settlements grew into villages, the homes of the animals were destroyed. So they were forced to move ever deeper into the forest.

The eldest raccoon child was happy—in her way—to find the forest so full of new faces. She was a complainer and very skilled at weeping, but as sometimes happens, her own family and the animals who knew her had gotten so accustomed to her lamentations that they no longer really listened to her. So she was always drifting about the forest, looking for listeners she had not met before.

One morning, she met a beaver she didn't know.

"You're new around here," she said.

"In the sense that you have just seen me," replied the beaver. "But I'm not new. I've been around in other places for quite some time. I'm from the south, and I had to leave the most extraordinary dam I've ever constructed because some human beings—"

"You'll find things difficult here," the raccoon said eagerly, not even aware she'd interrupted the beaver. "If you're like me, that is. I find *everything* so difficult. My brother and sister find everything easy. But some creatures have luck and others don't."

"That's true," said the beaver, staring at a heap of branches nearby.

"But it's not fair, is it?" asked the raccoon. And before the beaver could answer, she said, "Certain creatures just get picked on more than others."

"No, it's not fair," said the beaver.

"Only last week, when the wind blew so hard, an old bird's nest fell out of a tree and landed right on my head!"

"Dreadful!" exclaimed the beaver as he picked up a branch and began to gnaw on it.

"And I tripped over a paper wasp's nest and I got two horrible stings on my foot."

"Unheard of!" said the beaver.

"Even rabbits make fun of me because the fish in the brook steal grasshoppers right out of my paws when I'm washing them."

"Think of that!" said the beaver.

"Rabbits!" cried the raccoon. "Imagine what it is to be laughed at by rabbits!"

"Unthinkable," said the beaver.

"And last evening when we were all climbing that tree over there —see?—I fell the greatest distance any raccoon has ever fallen. That's because my eyes are poor at night. Can you believe such a thing? A raccoon with poor night vision?"

"I can believe it, and I do," said the beaver, turning the branch around and around in his paws. "You have terrible troubles. I might even say, *brilliant* troubles, better than any I've heard."

"Are you, by any chance, making fun of me?" asked the raccoon.

"Not at all," said the beaver, whose paws and teeth had been busy on the branch. Quite suddenly, and to the raccoon's surprise, the beaver blew into a hole he'd made in the branch. At once, a thin, sweet sound filled the clearing where they were standing.

"There!" said the beaver with satisfaction. "I've made you something nice." And he handed the branch to the raccoon. But it no longer looked like a mere branch. The beaver had smoothed it and rounded it, and it fit perfectly into the raccoon's paws.

"Where I come from in the south, we have a saying," explained the beaver. "When some animal has a long, sad tale to tell, one that he likes to tell over and over again, we say, 'Go play it on your old kazoo.' I can't make a kazoo. But I'm quite good at reeds. You'll find that with a little practice, you'll be able to *play* your tale, and instead of one listener, you'll have many. And all at the same time."

"But I don't know how to—" began the raccoon.

"Go listen to Jean-Paul," advised the beaver and turned away and headed for the brook nearby.

Even the little raccoon knew who Jean-Paul was, despite the fact she'd hardly heard a word said to her since the day she'd spoken *her* first word.

Jean-Paul had been born an otter like all other otters. But he had discovered at an early age that he was a musician. And all the animals in all the forests of the land knew that he was a great musician. For six months of every year, he gave concerts on his flute, and he had become rich and happy and rather plump.

The little raccoon knew he was somewhere in the forest, for he was to give a concert in a week. She set off in search of him and found him in the very center of the forest, surrounded by dozens and dozens of animals, some of whom brushed his beautiful coat, some of whom brought him tidbits to eat, and some of whom merely looked at him adoringly.

The little raccoon thought he must be the happiest creature on earth. His face shone with good feeling. He smiled constantly.

The raccoon watched the activities for a while. A badger was finishing the platform for Jean-Paul's concert.

"Splendid, *mon cher*," cried the big otter as he leaped onto the platform and strode about it. Jean-Paul had taken to using a foreign phrase now and then out of sheer high spirits.

Then he looked right at the little raccoon. "But who is this little soul watching me so shyly from the tree?" he asked, smiling.

She walked slowly toward the platform and held up her reed.

"I want to learn to play my troubles on this," she said timidly.

The otter laughed a great buttery laugh.

"What a lovely idea, *chérie!*" he cried. "Here, give it to me. Ah, the beaver from the south made this flute, didn't he? I know his work well."

He took the flute from her paws and drew in his breath and blew.

A waterfall of sound filled the forest, and then it was as though all the birds under the heavens were singing at once. On and on it went, that marvelous sound, even, it seemed, after Jean-Paul had handed the flute back to the little raccoon.

"Were you playing your troubles?" she asked.

"What an amusing thing to say, *ma petite,*" said Jean-Paul. "Playing my troubles! No, no. I was playing my delight—well—perhaps a very small trouble or two." He smiled so brightly it was impossible for the little raccoon to imagine that the great otter had a single trouble of any kind, not a ripple, not a drop of trouble.

"How will I ever learn," sighed the raccoon.

"I will teach you," said Jean-Paul. "I will give you three lessons. Then you must practice every day, no matter what, no matter if it storms or the earth rumbles or you hear the sounds of human creatures cutting down the trees and digging up the land." Then Jean-Paul turned to some of the animals who were sweeping the platform. *"Mes amis,"* he said, "resume all this tomorrow. I am going to take on a pupil."

For three days, Jean-Paul instructed the little raccoon. And she was so busy, she had no time to think or speak about her troubles. But once, just once, she began to tell Jean-Paul how her brother had hidden her favorite shiny stone. "We have no time for that," he said. "It is interesting, but not as interesting as what we are doing. Now. Don't lift your shoulders so high. You are breathing, not flying. Don't move your jaw when you blow."

"But there's no sound coming out," cried the raccoon. "It's only like leaves blowing."

"You must form your mouth into a smile. What? You can't smile?"

And she tried. But still the only sound that issued from the flute when she blew upon it was a thin, rustling noise such as a little snake might make crawling through a pile of dry leaves.

After that first lesson, the raccoon was so discouraged that she went and hid herself in an abandoned fox's lair. She did not have the heart to tell anyone about her new trouble. In the dark of the small cave, she told herself she would never be able to make a single sound come out of that stick of wood. After all, it *was* only a stick of wood!

She might not have gone back for her second lesson if she could have found someone to complain to the next morning about her brother—how he had dug a hole in the ground and covered it with twigs and leaves and then called to her, and how she had run to him and fallen right into that hole. But—just her luck—there wasn't a creature around, and so, dragging her feet and carrying the stick of wood, she went off to Jean-Paul.

"Wrong fingering," Jean-Paul said sternly. "You could not have forgotten since yesterday, *ma chérie!* Try again!"

"Do not honk!" he said.

"Don't breathe with your shoulders!" he said.

"Hold your flute more at an angle, please. It is not an egg you're eating. The flute is not an egg!" he said.

"Again!" he said. "And again!"

And then, unexpectedly, suddenly, a note flew out of the flute like a silver bird, and the little raccoon was astonished. Jean-Paul smiled, his cheeks like two apples.

"I knew you'd find it!" he said. *"Brava!"*

The rest of that day, the little raccoon was giddy with a strange new feeling that was painful and delicious and exhilarating all at the same time. It was not at all like the feeling she had when she found someone to listen to her bad-luck stories. She would have liked to practice her flute every minute, but Jean-Paul had said no, she must not practice every minute, only a few good minutes.

That night, her mother remarked, "Well—what's this? You're smiling!"

The little raccoon tried to stop, but she could feel the smile stirring her mouth like a little twig. "I'm practicing how to hold my mouth to play my flute," she said.

"It isn't everyone that the great otter would give lessons to," observed her mother proudly.

"He feels sorry for me because I have so many special troubles," said the little raccoon.

After that, everyone was silent.

The last lesson took place under a spruce tree whose thick needles sheltered the two animals from a heavy rain that had begun that morning.

When the little raccoon had wakened and heard the raindrops falling on leaves and trees, she had sighed. "Just my luck. . . ." she had said, hoping someone might overhear her. She hadn't known whether to go to the otter or not. But a field mouse had come with a message from Jean-Paul.

"You are to go for your third lesson even if the heavens split open," said the mouse, and he giggled, not being used to such florid language.

It was the best lesson of all. Jean-Paul took his own flute in his paws and played along with the little raccoon. But she was so excited she hardly knew what she was doing except that she was making dozens of mistakes. Yet the otter patted her shoulder and said, "Well done, *ma chérie!*"

"But my mistakes—" she said.

"But your effort," he said, "that is what is important. When I come back to your forest next year, I will expect you to be much improved, and I will expect you to have made up a song of your own to play for me and for all the animals."

"Oh!" cried the little raccoon. "But I can't! I couldn't! I don't know what to make up a song about! And I can't stand to be laughed at!"

"You will be able to," said the otter. "And no one will laugh at you, or else they will have to answer to me. Not every creature can make a silver bird fly out of the flute."

After the rain had stopped that afternoon, all the creatures of the forest gathered to hear Jean-Paul's concert. The little raccoon was there, too, listening to every sound, watching Jean-Paul's every move, amazed at her own understanding of what he was doing.

Later, when the forest was silent and heavy with twilight and the sleepiness of day animals, the field mouse came up to the little raccoon and said, "Jean-Paul says you must make up a song about living things."

"Living things?" she asked. "But what does that mean?"

The field mouse grinned. "I don't know," he said. "Maybe something like me."

For the next few months, the little raccoon thought only of her flute.

"What terrible new thing has happened to you?" a hedgehog would ask her, but she would look at him blankly and hurry off to a private place near the brook where she practiced. And at dinner, her sister would say, with a sly smile, "And who tripped you up, teased you, threw a stick at you, dropped a bird's nest on your head, hid your favorite stone, ate the berries you had gathered for your picnic, and stuck out a tongue at you today?"

But the little raccoon had nothing to tell. Her mind was full of the hard work she had done that day, and the hard work she would do tomorrow.

The leaves turned brown and dropped from the trees. The snow fell thickly, silently, and covered the ground. The brook froze over, and only now and then did a ragged bird come to sit on a bare oak branch. Food supplies dwindled away. Some animals slept throughout the days and nights in their tunnels and hollow tree trunks. But other animals perished from cold and from hunger. Sometimes the bark of a fox cracked the stillness.

In the hollow beneath the fallen tree, the raccoon family huddled together for warmth. And the little raccoon, although she could not actually play the flute, practiced thinking about it. And she held it close to her and moved her fingers over it even when she was so sleepy she could not keep awake, and they became as agile as separate little creatures.

Then the cold rains of early spring came, and they lasted so long it seemed the sky was draining away. One morning, pale sunlight fell over the forest. The ice on the brook began to melt. Pocked and yellow toadstools pushed through the dead, dank leaves. Patches of violets sprang up, and the vines sent out new runners. That day, the little raccoon went back to her private place by the brook. She discovered there that all her thinking had kept her memory of how to play as fresh as it had been when she'd crept beneath the fallen tree for the long winter rest. And she played all that day, the music she made curling and spinning throughout the forest until it was as though a great glistening web of sound touched every leaf of every tree.

The field mouse came to her and said, "We have all been listening to you, and although you are not as splendid a musician as Jean-Paul, you are very good."

No one in her family ever asked her now what new bad luck she had had. And none of the animals in the forest smirked at her when she passed them on her way to practice. She was thinking of her song now, and she paid no attention if one of her bright stones disappeared or a nest fell on her head.

Jean-Paul returned, at last, and the badger built a new platform for his concert, which was to be held on the longest day of summer.

The little raccoon, her flute in her paws—it was as smooth as water now, and polished to a fine sheen by her ceaseless efforts—went to the clearing where all the animals were gathering. Perhaps, she thought, Jean-Paul would not remember her. After all, he journeyed to so many places. But as soon as she had stepped into the clearing, he called out, "There you are, *mon chou!* How nice to see you! How pleased I am to see how well you hold the flute that was made for you by the beaver from the south!"

He kissed her on both cheeks and said, "After my concert is over, you will play for me." He waved at the crowd of animals. "And for all of them," he added.

The little raccoon said, "All winter I practiced thinking about my flute." But she said nothing of the cold, of the short, dark days, of how hungry she had been. Then she joined the audience and, along with them, sat spellbound while Jean-Paul played.

After, the great otter motioned her up to the platform.

"And now the little raccoon who has been working so hard all through the long bitter months will play her song for us," said Jean-Paul. "Tell us, what will your music say?"

The little raccoon whispered to Jean-Paul, "It is a very short song, and I will say it just to you."

But Jean-Paul turned her around so she faced all the animals.

"We all want to hear," he said firmly.

So the little raccoon stepped forward to the edge of the platform and spoke her song, which went like this:

> *I sing of all created things,*
> *Of all created things, and rings*
> *Of light, and rings of shade,*
> *And meadows sweet, and this sweet glade.*

Then she brought the flute to her lips and began to play. She played until darkness began to steal through the oak trees. Then it was time for all the animals to go home. She went home, too, the smile of the reed player on her mouth—although no one could see—and what she felt was the weight of her happiness.

But," said the duck after a minute or so, "did the little raccoon never complain anymore?"

"Oh, yes!" said the goose. "Once in a while. But that was no longer the *only* thing she did."

"Why is happiness a weight?" asked the duck.

For once the frogs didn't jump up with an answer.

"Well?" asked the duck. "Can't anyone tell me?"

"I can't," said the goose, sighing. "I think you'll have to find out for yourself."

"I should think happiness would weigh no more than a feather," said the duck, "a duck feather."

"Only a duck would think *that* was happiness," said the smallest frog scornfully.

Then the duck shook himself and asked, "Did the raccoon's song mean me, too? I'm a created thing, aren't I?"

"Yes," said the goose.

"And us, too!" cried all the frogs.

The duck shot them a dark look, but the goose nodded her head vigorously.

"Oh, yes," she said. "All of us."

"If only I'd had a great performer like Jean-Paul to manage," said the duck. "How different my life would have been!"

"I must go," said the goose with sudden urgency.

"Wait!" cried the duck. "Fate brought us together! Let me be your manager! You will become even more famous than the goose that laid the golden eggs!"

"I have my own fate," said the goose. And at that moment, the duck heard a distant honking that grew louder and louder until he saw, nearly overhead, a vast flock of geese flying in so perfect a V it was as though some huge and steady hand had drawn it across the sky.

There was a rush of air. The duck heard the great beat of the goose's wings, heard, too, a murmur, "Good-bye, my dears . . ." and then found himself nearly alone. Only the smallest frog still sat on a lily pad, gazing at him steadily.

"I've thought of taking tap-dancing lessons this winter," said the frog.

"Don't be ridiculous!" snapped the duck, then shook his head ashamedly. "Sorry to be so cross," he said. "It's only that I wish—"

"I know," said the frog. "But she really had to go with the rest of them."

"I suppose I'd better go myself," said the duck.

He squinted at the sky. Far away, he could still see the now ghostly V of the flock of Canadian geese flying south.

"Good luck," said the smallest frog.

"Likewise," said the duck. The frog jumped into the pond. The duck waited until the last ripple had disappeared, then he passed through the clump of reeds to the road.

Perhaps, he thought, he was the only creature alive without a fate.

At that second, just a few yards away, something leaped, something barked, and there was a flurry of white and dark and yellow fur. There, standing on its front paws, its back paws up in the air, was the strangest creature the duck had ever seen. Its long, thin tail hung over its back like a question mark. Its long, thin snout pointed straight down at the ground. It turned a cartwheel, then it did several handstands.

"Star material if I ever saw it," said the duck aloud, and hurried toward the other animal.

"Consider yourself signed up," said the duck. "That was a fine audition."

"I'm not auditioning," said the creature. "I always walk on my paws when I'm thinking." He stood upright and peered at the duck. "Don't you?" he asked.

"I suggest you stop thinking and we do some talking," said the duck.

"Why not do both at the same time?" asked the creature.

"In the first place," said the duck, "what on earth are you?"

"I am a coatimundi," replied the creature. "I can tell you where I'm from, but not where I am."

"We should get along well," said the duck, "since I can tell you where you are, but not where you are from."

"Brazil," said the coatimundi. "That's where I was born. My story is short, simple, and a touch tragic." His voice was very cheerful. "I was captured by a human being, crated, ticketed, and hurled onto the deck of a ship. I sailed for days and days and landed up in a great city, where I was uncrated and exhibited in a large cage. A family of human beings purchased me and brought me to some place in this area. This morning, I managed to slip away while they were all sleeping. I'd like to go home to my own country, but I don't know how to get there."

"Well—you're in the north country," said the duck. "And it's my guess, although geography is one of the few things I'm ignorant about, you have a long way to go to reach home. But I think I can help you accomplish that. I happen to be in the entertainment world. I'm a manager, in fact. And I've managed some of the most eminent performers in the land. After observing your acrobatics, I've decided to take you on. In time, we'll work our way south, perhaps all the way to Brazil."

"I'm not a performer," said the coatimundi. "I prefer a simple, solitary life."

"One is always alone onstage," said the duck reassuringly. "There's a large animal community just down this road. I might be able to arrange a booking for us this very day."

The coatimundi suddenly smiled. "Well, I have had a bit of luck, at last, haven't I? Meeting up with you?"

The duck was delighted to be thought even a bit of luck. But as he continued to tell the coatimundi about all the splendid possibilities that lay ahead for them, he kept glancing at the sky. The geese had long since disappeared. Oh well, he consoled himself, there's always one that gets away.